CHIL

JOHN BLACKBURN was born in 1923 in the village of Corbridge, England, the second son of a clergyman. Blackburn attended Haileybury College near London beginning in 1937, but his education was interrupted by the onset of World War II; the shadow of the war, and that of Nazi Germany, would later play a role in many of his works. He served as a radio officer during the war in the Mercantile Marine from 1942 to 1945, and resumed his education afterwards at Durham University, earning his bachelor's degree in 1949. Blackburn taught for several years after that, first in London and then in Berlin, and married Joan Mary Clift in 1950. Returning to London in 1952, he took over the management of Red Lion Books.

It was there that Blackburn began writing, and the immediate success in 1958 of his first novel, *A Scent of New-Mown Hay*, led him to take up a career as a writer full time. He and his wife also maintained an antiquarian bookstore, a secondary career that would inform some of Blackburn's work, including the bibliomystery *Blue Octavo* (1963). *A Scent of New-Mown Hay* typified the approach that would come to characterize Blackburn's twenty-eight novels, which defied easy categorization in their unique and compelling mixture of the genres of science fiction, horror, mystery, and thriller. Many of Blackburn's best novels came in the late 1960s and early 1970s, with a string of successes that included the classics *A Ring of Roses* (1965), *Children of the Night* (1966), *Nothing but the Night* (1968; adapted for a 1973 film starring Christopher Lee and Peter Cushing), *Devil Daddy* (1972) and *Our Lady of Pain* (1974). Somewhat unusually for a popular horror writer, Blackburn's novels were not only successful with the reading public but also won widespread critical acclaim: the *Times Literary Supplement* declared him 'today's master of horror' and compared him with the Grimm Brothers, while the *Penguin Encyclopedia of Horror and the Supernatural* regarded him as 'certainly the best British novelist in his field' and the *St James Guide to Crime & Mystery Writers* called him 'one of England's best practicing novelists in the tradition of the thriller novel'.

By the time Blackburn published his final novel in 1985, much of his work was already out of print, an inexplicable neglect that continued until Valancourt began republishing his novels in 2013. John Blackburn died in 1993.

BY JOHN BLACKBURN

A Scent of New-Mown Hay (1958)*
A Sour Apple Tree (1958)
Broken Boy (1959)*
Dead Man Running (1960)
The Gaunt Woman (1962)
Blue Octavo (1963)*
Colonel Bogus (1964)
The Winds of Midnight (1964)
A Ring of Roses (1965)*
Children of the Night (1966)*
The Flame and the Wind (1967)*
Nothing but the Night (1968)*
The Young Man from Lima (1968)
Bury Him Darkly (1969)*
Blow the House Down (1970)
The Household Traitors (1971)*
Devil Daddy (1972)*
For Fear of Little Men (1972)
Deep Among the Dead Men (1973)
Our Lady of Pain (1974)*
Mister Brown's Bodies (1975)
The Face of the Lion (1976)*
The Cyclops Goblet (1977)*
Dead Man's Handle (1978)
The Sins of the Father (1979)
A Beastly Business (1982)*
The Book of the Dead (1984)
The Bad Penny (1985)*

* Available or forthcoming from Valancourt Books

CHILDREN OF THE NIGHT

BY

JOHN BLACKBURN

VALANCOURT BOOKS

Children of the Night by John Blackburn
First published London: Jonathan Cape, 1966
First Valancourt Books edition 2014

Published by Valancourt Books, Richmond, Virginia
Publisher & Editor: James D. Jenkins
20th Century Series Editor: Simon Stern, University of Toronto
http://www.valancourtbooks.com

All Valancourt Books publications are printed on acid free paper
that meets all ANSI standards for archival quality paper.

ISBN 978-1-941147-10-8 *(trade paperback)*

Set in Dante MT 11/13.6
Cover by M. S. Corley

CHAPTER ONE

'If this old bitch blew up with the *Bedford*, the world would be rid of a prize load of scum.' Captain James Kendal, master of the salvage vessel, *Dalecrest*, leaned against the wheel-house bulkhead, scowling down at his crew, and then, for the benefit of the chief officer beside him, added, 'Present company excepted, of course, Mr. Sweatenham.'

Yes, they really were a bunch, he thought. Dirty, idle, inefficient and, apart from the two divers, there wasn't a proper salvage man amongst them. Insubordinate too. When he'd torn a strip off Daniels, the bos'n, for coming aboard drunk the other night, the man had given him a stupid smirk and said he was sorry if he'd overstayed his welcome on the ship. One more crack like that and Daniels would have earned himself a bad entry in his discharge book.

But after all, what could one expect from a rotten tub like this *Dalecrest?* Twenty-three years old, slung together during the war, with outdated equipment, and accommodation that was primitive, to say the least. Just the command for somebody like himself who should have retired years ago, if he hadn't married a young and extravagant wife to run through his savings. Kendal turned up his collar against the cold air that was blowing in from the sea and stared across the bay. In the north, brown moorland hills stretched away to Scotland, and to the south was Dunstonholme village with the evening sun high above the little ruined castle behind it. Doubtless the view was very lovely, but he was in no mood to appreciate scenic beauty at the moment.

'Just another eight minutes to go, Mister – if they've managed to set the fuse correctly, of course.' Kendal consulted an inscribed gold watch which had been presented to him for picking up survivors from a French trawler when he was second mate on the *Fort Malaine.* Half a mile away a yellow marker buoy was rising and falling on the swell and, below it, acid should be eating through a wire. When the wire snapped a hundredweight of explosive would rip open the wreck of the American liberty ship, *Samson J. Bedford*.

'Look at the fools. You'd think there was gold bullion or pirate treasure down there.' All the crew who were not actively on duty had crowded forward and were watching the marker with an air of holiday excitement. 'They're like kids waiting for a ruddy fair to open.

'Damn this fog, though.' It was thickening out to sea and even the nearest of the Feyne Islands was hardly visible. Just another thing to hold them back, Kendal thought. From the day they'd left the Thames he had had a strange feeling that things were going to go wrong – a premonition that Fate was against him, and the subsequent events appeared to prove him right. A week's delay at Tyneport because of engine trouble, an anchor jamming as soon as they reached Dunstonholme, and the faulty air-pump that had almost killed his second diver. Now, at the very moment when they needed good visibility, the wind had veered to the east and the fog was closing in.

'Latest Met. report, sir.' As though in answer to his thoughts, the radio operator appeared on the bridge and handed him a sheet of paper. He was barely nineteen years old, but two trips as a junior with the Orient line had given him a jaunty superior manner which Kendal found infuriating.

'The pundits say it's going to get pretty thick later on, but I wouldn't be too sure, sir.' He nodded towards the sunset. ' "Red sky at night – shepherd's delight," and all that sort of thing.'

'Shepherd's?' Kendal snorted as he read through the forecast. 'Are you a bloody shepherd, Sparks? It's sailor's delight, as long as you're on this ship, and don't you forget it.'

'Of course, sir.' The boy was obviously quite unconcerned by the rebuff. 'Is it all right if I stay up here and watch the fun for a bit?'

'Yes, as long as you keep out of my way.' Kendal glanced across at the shore. At least the Dunstonholme harbour-master had managed to deter sightseers and, apart from a fishing boat far out to starboard, the bay was deserted.

Shepherd's delight, he thought. Fun, indeed! There was no

shred of romance about this job. All they had to do was to open a coffin which should have been left in peace if the *Samson J. Bedford* hadn't been carrying pig lead, and with the present world shortage of lead its recovery might just show the *Dalecrest*'s owners a profit. A damned small profit after all the delays they'd had so far. Kendal suddenly seemed to have another premonition that more mishaps were on their way.

It was in July '43 that the *Bedford* had gone down. She was anchored in the bay, waiting to join an east coast convoy, when a Dornier bomber driven back from Tynecastle by the barrage had spotted her. The pilot had come in low and his first bomb had hit her amidships, splitting the welded hull like a can so that she turned turtle and sank immediately. Now the wreck lay under twenty fathoms, wedged in a rock fissure, and he had to open it up for a thousand tons of pig lead. Very exciting!

Only four minutes to go. There was a perfectly accurate clock on the bulkhead, but it gave Kendal pleasure to pull out his watch again. The very feel of the heavy, gleaming metal made him think of the days when he wasn't so tired and bad-tempered and apprehensive.

'Ring down to the engine room and see that they're on their toes, Mr. Sweatenham. I want to be anchored over her before that fog reaches us.' What was that odd sense of dread that kept flicking across his thoughts? Old age? Too much imagination? Too many failures and defeats in the past?

Three and a half minutes. He scanned the shore, half expecting to see a boat put out from the harbour and head towards them, but the area was still quite clear. Two minutes – one and a half – one and a quarter. . . . There was a sound like an enormous sigh, followed by a cheer from the men in the bows. A blister of brown water reared up over the buoy for a moment and then cascaded back in rivulets. As was to be expected from equipment supplied by the *Dalecrest*'s owners, the fuse had gone off early. Still, the charge should have done its work and, in the morning, they could start to recover the cargo.

'Well, so far so good, Mr. Sweatenham.' Kendal lifted the telegraph handle and rang for half speed. The old ship shuddered and heaved for a moment and then began to creep slowly forward. The sea breeze was getting stronger now and the fog much closer, pouring over the surface of the water like smoke. At least the marker had stayed in position to guide them through, and, as they approached, a cluster of bubbles burst around it, released from some air pocket in the wreck. He walked to the wing of the flying bridge and looked over the side. The bottom of the bay was rock and the water had remained fairly clear.

There was no floating timber, of course. It was almost twenty-three years since the *Bedford* had gone down and the hatch covers would have been waterlogged ages ago. Plenty of dead fish, though. Mackerel, rock salmon, flatties, and a couple of big conger eels, both of them five foot long if an inch. And, over there, a seal floating on its back. The poor devil looked quite peaceful but, as they passed, he could see that its belly had been torn open by the explosion.

But no gulls. Not a bird in sight. Surely that was strange? Flocks of them had been round the ship all day, and it was over five minutes since the wreck had been blown. They had flown off when they heard the blast, but one would have expected them to have come back and been after those fish by now. Yes, very odd. He could see them swirling over the headland to the south-west.

Time to stop engines. He nodded to Sweatenham, whose hand was already on the telegraph, and the ship slid silently towards the marker. Her bows were almost in fog, and for a moment he considered going forward to supervise the lowering of the anchor, but at once dismissed the idea as unnecessary and bad for discipline. Baxter, his second mate, was no nautical genius, but reliable enough.

'God, but it's cold, sir!' He turned as the radio officer crossed to his side. The boy's voice had lost all its usual jauntiness and his face looked drawn and pinched as the fog closed around it.

'Yes, it's cold enough, son.' Normally Kendal would have resented the interruption, but the fog really was icy. A bitter, biting cold that sent tremors through his body and made him think of old seamen's superstitions: ghost ships off Cape Horn, the great

Norway maelstrom, and the Kraken roaring up to the surface to die.

They must be getting pretty close to the marker, though. He should hear the anchor chain go at any moment. Too close. What were the fools doing? From forward there was a dull crash and a scraping sound as the bows hit the buoy and started to pass over its cable.

'Mr. Baxter.' He cupped his hands into a trumpet. 'What the hell are you up to? Let go that anchor at once.' He lurched slightly, feeling the deck shudder under his feet and hearing the engines burst into life again. The chief engineer must have taken leave of his senses when they hit the buoy and thrown them into reverse. Unless he was lucky, the cable would be round his propeller in a second.

And then it happened. The beat of the engines was suddenly joined by another noise. A deep humming roar in the back of his head and at the same instant the fog appeared to thicken into a solid, like old foul rags being wrapped round his face to blind and choke him. The cold was like nothing he had ever experienced or imagined, and with it came fear. During the war Kendal had spent four days on a raft with only a corpse for company, but he had not felt so alone and helpless as he did at that moment. The deck vibrated as the engines built up to full power, but much louder than the noise of the engines was the roar in his head which was changing to a voice that shouted – 'Get out.'

'Sir – please, sir – please, Captain. . . .' The operator lurched drunkenly against him and clutched his arm. 'Something's there, sir – down there . . .'

'You could be right, boy.' Kendal pushed him aside, and he knew that there was no 'could' about it. There really was something near them, something at the bottom of the bay which the explosion had disturbed. He had no idea what it was, but he sensed that it was very old and hostile and incredibly dangerous. He also knew that there was only one way to deal with it, and the responsibility was his. He was the ship master, the *Dalecrest* was his command and it was up to him to save her. He staggered to the wheel-house with the voice in his head shouting, 'Get out – get out – get out . . .'

The quartermaster was stretched out on the deck apparently unconscious and Kendal grasped the wheel. The spokes were like ice in his hands, but the rudder started to bite almost at once. Beside him, Sweatenham was leaning against the telegraph. There was no hint of intelligence on his face but he was holding the handle at 'full ahead'.

'Get out – we must get out to sea.' Kendal muttered the words aloud. 'Far out to sea.' He still had not the slightest idea of what he was running from, but he knew it was there all right: a thing that was coming closer at every second and which could destroy him utterly if he didn't run. Something old and hideous and obscene: a blight moving up from the depths.

'Out – out – out.' The fog blanketed the wheel-house windows, but the signal gun on Paul's Point showed him the mouth of the bay. The *Dalecrest* heaved and pitched as she met the rough water over the bar and the engines thudded steadily on. Soon Kendal ceased to hear them. He didn't even hear the gun. All he could hear was that screaming, shouting inner voice that told him to 'Get out – get out – get out.'

CHAPTER TWO

'NORTH SEA TRAGEDY . . . STILL NO EXPLANATION.' Colonel Hector Keith steadied his newspaper against the wind, and leaned comfortably back in the wheelchair.

'After a two-day search by ships and aircraft, survivors are yet to be found from the salvage vessel, *Dalecrest*, and the coastal tanker, *Grimsby Lass*, which were lost off the Outer Feyne Islands last Monday night.' The colonel smiled slightly. He enjoyed reading about other people's misfortunes.

The only eyewitnesses of the disaster were the keepers of the Mary-feyne light-house who radioed the alarm, after hearing an explosion and seeing a huge glow on the horizon. From their account it seems clear that the two vessels collided in the dense fog that covered the area, and that the *Grimsby Lass*, which was carrying five hundred tons of high octane petrol, caught fire and exploded.

What the *Dalecrest* was doing among the Outer Feynes remains a mystery. For the previous two days she had been engaged in salvage operations in Dunstonholme Bay, and at about ten o'clock in the evening was seen to proceed out to sea. A number of persons witnessed her departure, and Commander William Clarke, R.N. Retd, stated as follows:

'The *Dalecrest* blew the wreck at approximately twenty-two hundred hours, being hove to half a mile away from it, and then proceeded towards the marker buoy, intending, as I thought, to anchor beside it for the night.

'The fog closed in at that moment and it was very difficult to see exactly what happened, but the vessel appeared to pass right over the marker and head for the shore. For a moment I thought that she would run herself on to the Sparbell Rocks, but she suddenly swung round and headed out to the mouth of the bay. I felt that her captain's behaviour was erratic, to say the least.' [Keith snorted. Trust that spineless fellow Billy Clarke to put it mildly. In his own mind, drink was the obvious explanation.]

The dearth of wreckage found near the scene of the explosion suggests . . .

The colonel closed the paper and pushed it down the side of his chair. He had spoken to some of the lifeboat's crew only yesterday, and he knew all about that wreckage. Some floating timber, a couple of upturned rafts, a dead man, part of a dead man, an unrecognizable thing which might have been a dead man, drifting away into the fog, and a few lifebelts. The two ships must have been ripped open by the explosion and sunk instantaneously, dragging their people with them.

Yes, fire and water, he thought. Nasty ways to die. Not nearly the worst, though. Not as bad as healthy old age. The organs slowing down and beginning to decay together: lungs, kidneys, liver, and at last the heart. Horrible! As always happened when he considered death, a little tic started to beat in the colonel's forehead, and he swung round in the chair.

'Come on, you idle man. It's almost four o'clock already. Put some beef into it.'

'I'm doing me best, sir. I can't do more than that.' The hill was very steep, and Corporal Joe Bates was almost bent double behind the handles. The sun was hot too, and he longed to stop and wipe the sweat from his forehead, but he knew what his employer would say about that.

You rotten old swine, he thought. We could take the car to the top of the lane, but that wouldn't do for you. No, not on your life. 'Get the chair out of the boot, Bates, and we'll have an airing. Do us both a power of good.' For two pins, I'd leave you and go to my sister.

Yes, I'll go to Betty and the old swine can die in a home. He's frightened of that. He knows that they don't stand any nonsense in those places, however much you pay them. There'll be no more 'Three bags full, Colonel Keith', then. No more ringing his bell morning, noon and night. No more riding about in this blasted chair. I'll go to Betty, and he won't kill me like he killed the Missus.

It made Bates feel better to think like that, but he knew it was an idle threat. His sister had four children and no room for him. Besides there was the money: all that money which was going to keep him in comfort for the rest of his life after Keith died. The memory of the will form glowed before his eyes as Bates struggled upward.

'I Hector Charles Keith, Colonel R.A., Retd., do hereby declare that this is my last will and testament . . .' A thousand to the regiment, a thousand to his club, and the rest to his cousin at Bournemouth. Apart from the bit that mattered, of course. The bit in the middle.

'To my manservant Joseph Bates I leave the sum of twenty thousand pounds provided that he is in my service at the time of my death and also provided that I am certified to have died from natural causes.'

There it was, locked away in the desk and drawn up all legal and proper, though the swine had been too mean to employ a lawyer. Bates had witnessed it himself with the cleaning woman, so he knew it was in order. Twenty thousand pounds! Clever of him to add that bit about natural causes. Without that, he'd have a good mind to let go of the chair right now and give him a free ride downhill.

Leaning back against the cushions, Colonel Keith was enjoying himself. He knew what Bates's thoughts would be and they amused him greatly: so did the knowledge that the man would go on working himself to the bone with no chance of a reward at the end of it.

Ignorant lout! Witnessed the will himself, and didn't realize that that cut him out: he wouldn't get a penny. 'Hah-hah-hah.' The colonel cackled with senile glee and then swung round, demanding more speed.

No, that was wrong. He should just sit quietly and not get excited. Any exertion was stupid and dangerous at his age. It taxed the heart, as that young fool, Dr. Allen, kept telling him. Keith lifted a gloved hand and adjusted the shawl around his shoulders. It was getting on for midsummer and the sun was warm, but one couldn't be too careful. He would be eighty-four next birthday. Another bout of 'flu like last year . . .

He wouldn't think about that now. Emotion was bad for him too. He should just take things easy and enjoy the view. He'd always liked that long brown sweep of the moors, the purple cloud in the south which was Tynecastle, and to his left, the bay curving out to sea. Just over there was the wreck-buoy still bobbing on the swell. Drink was the cause of that captain's behaviour all right. He must have been roaring drunk. His crew had been a drunken bunch as well, by all accounts. Three of them had been causing trouble in the village only last Saturday, and that wretched fellow, Constable Rutter, hadn't had the guts to lock them up. Good riddance to some very bad rubbish.

Still it was a bit of a mystery. Surely one or two of the officers would have been sober enough to take command? There had been a lot of mysteries along this stretch of coast, if it came to that: the legend of a Roman cohort that had marched north on a punitive expedition and vanished somewhere out on the hills; that crazy medieval sect, the Children of Paul, who had sailed out from Dunstonholme in 1300 and been drowned; the story of the haunted railway cutting. And now this salvage boat. Though the sun was warm, Keith felt a sudden chill.

Why didn't Bates get a move on? Great strapping, hulking fellow who wished him dead, and was for ever grumbling and suggesting they should drive up in the car. Why should they, if he enjoyed going in the chair? Nobody respected his wishes these days. All of them tried to thwart and belittle him: the parson who refused to let him read the lessons, the doctor trying to cut down his whisky, his son, Hugh, who wrote rubbishy verse, and hadn't even been to see him since Madge died. Hugh would have his eyes opened when the will was read. Damn Hugh! Damn them all!

Almost up to Milkwell Burn now. The local people called it a waterfall which was a stupid boast, because it was just a trickle of peaty water dripping over a boulder and then disappearing through a crack in the ground. The moor around here was supposed to contain hundreds of caves and underground waterways, but no one ever seemed to explore them.

Brrr! It was getting cold, though, apart from the cloud over Tynecastle and a little haze in the north, the sky was clear. Keith pulled a flask from his picnic basket and raised it to his lips, choking slightly as the neat spirit burned his throat. Whatever Tom Allen might say, whisky in moderation never did anybody any harm, and it was the best thing in the world for his catarrh. He had to watch that. He didn't want to go out like Madge.

What a stupid, foolhardy woman Madge had been! Out gardening in November without a coat, catching a chill, leaving him. Selfish and wicked of her too. After all, she was the younger and stronger of the two, and everybody had known that he was the invalid, and bound to die first. It had been her duty to take care of herself, so she could look after him till the end.

But he mustn't think about Madge any more. She was dead and the least thought of death troubled him. Fire, water, burial. Bodies rotting in earth and liquid, or melting in flames. Horrible!

Waterfall indeed! Keith stared contemptuously at the stream. A miserable brown dribble on the rocks which trickled across the road and finally vanished through a hole on the other side. There was something rather sinister about it too, like that brook up on the border that had been choked with Scottish corpses after Flodden. What did they call it locally? 'Horrid Gutter.'

Being buried alive would be the worst thing of all. Lying deep at the bottom of a shaft with tons of rock and soil piled on top of you. Silence, pitch darkness and bitter, bitter cold. Again a shiver ran through his body. The wind really was getting chilly and it had nothing to do with his imagination.

'Very well, Bates. I've changed my mind and we'll turn back now.' They had reached the crest of the hill, and the lane had started to run down towards Dunstonholme Village. A few yards farther on was the gate by which he liked to eat his tea and look at the view. The bay spread out below him, with the Inner Feynes like grey billiard tables on the water and Paul's Point where those crazy fanatics had met their deserts over six hundred years ago. Usually he enjoyed it very much, but today it suddenly seemed hostile and threatening, and he just wanted to go home: back to the car, back to his house, and back to a warm bed. He had to get away from this cold wind which was attacking every nerve in his body, and the sense of impending disaster that came with it. There was a trickle of icy sweat on his forehead and his hands tightened around the tiller.

'Didn't you hear me, Bates?' The chair was still trundling gently on along the slope. The fellow must be becoming deaf as well as lazy. 'I said I wanted you to take me home.' He swung round and his voice rose to a scream. 'For the love of God, Bates!'

Bates was no longer near him. He was fifteen yards away or more, standing in the centre of the lane, with the stream trickling over his feet, and his hands pressed against his eyes. At every second the chair gathered speed.

Keith started to swing the tiller towards the side of the road. The only thing to do was to tip himself over and chance a fall, but within inches of the verge he knew that he couldn't do it. The thought of the tarmac smashing against his old, frail body was hideous and obscene. He pulled on to the crown and went down with his scarf blowing behind him and a thin constant scream at his lips.

So he rolled on to his death. Slowly at first, and then faster and faster, as the slope steepened. Ten miles an hour, fifteen, twenty. Down past Blyegate Farm, where a sheep dog rushed out, snapping at the wheels. Down past two small children picking flowers who turned and looked admiringly at him, as though thinking he were engaged in some heroic sport. Down past Jessop's paddock, with the old shorthorn bull bellowing over the wall. Down towards the village and the place where the road turned sharply left before joining the main road. The front wheel bounded madly on the rough surface, but somehow held its course. It couldn't take the bend, though. The chair shot over the verge, hit the protecting wall at thirty miles an hour and stopped dead. Colonel Keith didn't stop. Like a fighter pilot ejected from his aircraft, he rose gracefully from the seat, appeared to hang suspended in space for a moment, and then plunged head first into the village square some forty feet below.

CHAPTER THREE

'It was God, eh? God told you to let go of that chair?' Sergeant Fenwick of the County Constabulary was looking in the direction of Bates, but he scarcely saw him. He scarcely saw the dingy interview room, if it came to that. In his mind's eye he was standing on the bridge of a destroyer as she tore out to sea, with her ensign stiff in the breeze, white foam at the bows and the engines vibrating beneath his feet.

'That was the only reason, Bates? You were feeling quite well till you reached the top of the hill?' Fenwick stifled a sigh. A week ago, two unusually talented teenage delinquents named 'Iron' Rails and Billy Dander had escaped from a Borstal institution and he had been put on their trail. They were reported to have been seen at the holiday resort of Blymouth that morning, and by lunch-time a twenty thousand pound catamaran was found to be missing from the yacht basin. Rails was a keen member of the Young Communist League, and it was thought that they might be attempting to reach Russia in the hope of gaining asylum there. Fenwick would dearly have loved to have been aboard one of the naval units detailed for the pursuit, but with a mixture of malice and selfishness the Inspector had gone himself and sent him off to Dunstonholme to investigate Colonel Keith's death.

'You're still not pleading ill health, Bates? You just say that God told you to do it?' He frowned at the man's garbled statement on the desk. When he first arrived at Dunstonholme, he had imagined he might have a cunning murderer hiding under the defence of insanity to deal with, but that thought had faded after five minutes with Bates. The man was just a poor half-wit, and 'unfit to plead' would be the only possible ending.

It was all very disappointing, though there might be some useful publicity for Fenwick in the case, for the colonel's end had been dramatic, to say the least. It was market day in Dunstonholme and he had arrived in the village square like a bolt from the blue, landing on a stall and breaking his neck and a large stock of plaster animals at the same instant. Through the door, Fenwick could hear Mr. Solly Black, the owner of the stall, stridently inquiring who would reimburse him for his losses.

'Somebody will have to pay for them, Officer, that's what I say. Five standard cats – three large de-luxe cats – they've got genuine velvet ribbons round their necks – eight poodles; six large giraffes – a very popular line that – two standard alsatians . . .'

'That's right, sir. I've been thinking about it, it must have been Him.' Bates blinked, as though coming out of a deep sleep, and nodded vigorously. 'There's no other explanation. God told me to kill him.'

'I see.' Fenwick finished the sketch of a destroyer he had been scribbling on his pad. He hadn't got the bows quite right, but there was a fine feeling of speed and menace about it. 'And what did God say to you, Bates?'

'Oh, he didn't actually say anything, Sergeant. You don't understand what it was like. I didn't either at first. I agreed with Dr. Allen, that I must have had some sort of fainting fit.' He looked at a tall young man who was sitting on a bench against the far wall. 'Then you told me about the will, and I knew it was God.'

'Thank you, Sergeant. That's very kind of you.' He accepted one of Fenwick's cigarettes and pulled hard at it.

'It happened like this, you see, gentlemen. I was pretty tired pushing him up that hill. It's steep in places, and he's no light weight, is he? Fifteen stone, I think you said, Doctor. The sun was hot too, and I wanted to stop for a bit and wipe the sweat off me face, but I knew what the old swine would have to say about that.

'Oh, yes, I hated him, Sergeant Fenwick, and I don't mind admitting it. Fifteen years I worked for the colonel, and he treated me like a dog after his wife died. Ringing his bell all the time, making me push him about in the chair, and cutting down me wages to a quid a week, because he'd left me all that money and said I'd be in clover when he was gone. That's exactly what he said, gentlemen. "You work hard, Bates, and that will stays as it is. You'll be in clover, once I'm under the sod."' Rather horribly a single tear trickled down his left cheek.

'And now you tell me that the will is no good because I witnessed it myself. I won't get a penny! That's what shows me it was God, Doctor. He set me free. He told me that I had to escape. Without him I'd have gone on slaving for Keith for years.'

'Yes, I appreciate that, Joe.' Tom Allen glanced towards the door. Mr. Black was almost screaming as he recited his losses. 'Eight standard penguins — nine super de-luxe alsatians – marvellous consignment that was. They've got real fur tails that wag when you pat 'em. Three polar bears . . .'

'But I think that Sergeant Fenwick would like to know exactly what happened to make you let go of the chair. You say that you didn't hear a voice?'

'No, there was no voice, sir. It was just a sort of feeling.' Bates closed his eyes as he tried to concentrate. 'I was very hot when we got to the top of the hill, and I remember looking at the stream which runs across the road and thinking how cool and pleasant it was. Then, all at once, the air seemed to go cold. Yes, cold as ice it was, and something seemed to happen to my eyes. I couldn't see properly, and . . .' He broke off and the cigarette fell from his hand and lay smouldering on the desk.

'And what, Bates?' Fenwick reached out and stubbed the cigarette in his ash-tray. 'What happened after you couldn't see?

'Well, I got frightened, sir. Terrified I was. I've been frightened before, of course. Cut off in Malaya we was once, with the Japs all around us. I was frightened then because I knew how they treated their prisoners, but it was nothing like this.

'This was awful, sir. I suddenly thought that I was being buried alive; trapped at the bottom of a deep shaft with tons of rock about to fall on me. I knew that if I didn't get out quick, I'd rot there for ever.'

'And that was the moment when you let go of the chair?' As Tom spoke an outside door banged and there was a sudden silence in the next room. Solly Black must have despaired of Constable Rutter's assistance and taken his losses elsewhere.

'I suppose it must have been, Doctor, but I can't be certain. All I can really be sure about is the cold, and the blindness, and the feeling that I'd be trapped if I didn't get away. I think I stood by the stream for a few seconds, and then I ran off down the hill. I got about fifty yards or so, when I tripped over and fell. I must have been laid out for a bit, but when I came round, everything was back to normal. The sun was warm, my eyes were all right, and I didn't feel frightened any more. I went back to where I'd left the colonel and he was gone. You know the rest of it, Doctor?'

'I know the rest of it, Joe.' Tom recalled the scene in the village square. A streamer reading 'BLACK'S BARGAIN CENTRE' swaying above the crowd. Two dogs barking, a woman screaming hysterically and, when he finally managed to push his way through, Colonel Keith's face leering up at him from the shattered pottery.

'But are you sure it was God, and not the Devil who gave you those strange feelings?'

'Of course it was God, Doctor.' Bates nodded again. 'How could it be anybody else? The Devil can only tell lies, and this was all true. I was being trapped, wasn't I? For years I'd slaved for old Keith, but God set me free at last. Without that vision of His, it might have gone on for the rest of me life. Like with Saint Paul on the road to Damascus, it was. A blinding white light that showed me the truth.

'And not a penny I'll get, you say? Not a single ruddy penny?'

'No, I'm afraid not, Joe.' Tom felt great sympathy for him. The colonel had been his patient for some time and he knew the life Bates had led. He also realized that there was no point in continuing the interview, and glanced across at Fenwick.

'Well, thank you very much, Bates.' The sergeant got up and opened the door. 'That will be all for the time being, and Constable Rutter will look after you. I expect there will be a nice supper

before long.' He smiled as Bates shambled slowly past him and
closed the door.

'So much for that, eh.' Once again the image of that hurtling
destroyer flashed across Fenwick's mind. The inspector would be
enjoying himself and they would probably have caught up with
the catamaran by now. 'What about it, Doctor? Is he completely barmy, or is there a
chance that he made it all up? Pushed the old boy down the hill
deliberately, and then invented this vision idea to support an
insanity plea?'

'I'd say that was highly unlikely, though I'm not a psychiatrist,
of course.' Tom glanced at his watch. He had promised to take his
wife out that evening and time was getting on.

'If you are stupid enough to witness a will from which you hope
to benefit, you'd hardly have the sense to concoct a complicated
defence. Also remember that Bates only stood to gain from Keith's
will if he died from natural causes. I wouldn't describe that death
dive as natural.

'In any case, why go to all the trouble? All Joe had to say was
that he had a sudden attack of giddiness or a black-out, and when
he came to, the chair had gone. I know his medical history; there is
a slight aorta weakness, and I'd have backed him up.

'No, I'd say that Joe Bates was telling the exact truth.'

'The act of God!' Fenwick raised his eyebrows. 'You're not
serious, Dr. Allen?'

'Yes, I'm serious in a way, Mr. Fenwick. Even the most hide-
bound materialist pays his respects to the supernatural at times.
Don't you walk round ladders now and then? Though I don't go to
church, I turn over the silver in my pocket when I see a new moon,
and touch my hat to magpies.' He smiled apologetically.

'Yes, I think Joe Bates was telling the truth, as far as he can
see it. He's an old man, getting on for seventy, and Keith was no
featherweight. It's been a very hot day, and that hill is pretty steep.
At the top, one of two things happened. Either he had a black-out,
or Keith abused him once too often and he let go of the chair. It's
perfectly natural for somebody of his mentality to attribute a slight
stroke or an act of anger to some supernatural force. Remember

that he was quite prepared to accept the black-out idea till you told him that the will was invalid.'

'You mean that, when he realized that Keith had tricked him, he put his death down to some divine retribution? As a means of quietening his conscience, if he really did kill him deliberately.'

'Possibly, but don't think you'll get a murder, or even a man-slaughter charge to stick, Sergeant. Not if my evidence counts at all. I know how Joe Bates was treated by Keith, and if it's necessary, I'll be in the box to swear that he could have had a stroke.' Tom looked at his watch again and stood up. Mary would be leaving the house soon, and they had arranged to meet at the Crown and have a drink before going on for a meal in Tynecastle. The Crown was usually quite amusing on market days, and they might run into that man, Moldon Mott, who was staying there; interesting chap when he wasn't talking about himself all the time.

'But who knows, Mr. Fenwick?' he said. 'Perhaps it really was an act of God. "Quem deus vult perdere prius dementat." After all, if you're foolish enough to abuse somebody who is holding your wheelchair at the top of a hill, I would say you were tempting providence quite a bit.' He held out his hand and smiled.

'And now, I'll be on my way. This should have been my day off, and I intend to enjoy what's left of it. Let me know if there's anything else I can do, and remember that I'll be for the defence if you make a charge.'

'Goodbye for the present.' He turned and walked through into the little reception hall. At the desk, two children, Janet and Alice Baker, identical twins, were telling their story to a policewoman.

'We thought it was all a game at the beginning, Miss. As though the old gentleman was having a lark. Ever so funny he looked, with his scarf blowing out behind him.' Alice did the talking, but Janet gripped her hand tightly and nodded at the end of each sentence.

'He was going fast too, and making a kind of screeching noise. When he got to the farm, Mr. Jessop's old dog came out and ran barking beside the chair, and we ran after him. Right down to the bend he went and bounced over the grass till he hit the wall. A terrible bang the chair made, Miss, and he shot up out of it like a Jack-in-the-Box. We climbed up on to the wall to look down and . . .' Simultaneously and without warning Alice and Janet burst into tears.

'No, I'm very sorry, gentlemen, but there is really nothing that I can tell you.' Two youthful reporters from the local paper stepped in front of him as Tom left the police station.

'Yes, I knew Colonel Keith quite well, but he was one of my patients, and I can answer no questions about his character. If you are writing an obituary, why not concentrate on his service career? I believe he won an M.C. in Italy during the First World War.

'The actual cause of death.' He looked across the square. There was a lot of blood-stained sand by the shattered stall, and beside it Solly Black was reciting his losses to a most unsympathetic audience. 'T' hell with yer blasted ornaments. 'Ave a bit of respect for the dead, can't yer?'

'I'd have thought that was obvious enough to anybody, gentlemen. Colonel Keith broke his neck on a consignment of plaster animals. And now, if you will excuse me please.' Tom pushed past them and hurried on.

It was pretty late. He had arranged to meet Mary at seven-fifteen, and the church clock showed almost that now, though the sun was still high in the sky. Only a few more days to midsummer. The heather wasn't out, of course, but some trick of light gave the near-by hills a deep purple tinge which contrasted beautifully with the pale green of the sea. Tom glanced through the railings as he passed the church. There were some interesting monuments in the churchyard, all of them somehow connected with the sea, which often brought visitors to the village at week-ends. A shattered spar in a stone shrine: TO THE CREW OF THE BRIG, THREE BROTHERS, WHO PERISHED DURING THE GREAT GALE, DECEMBER 1843 . . . A cross with an anchor chain twined around it: IN MEMORY OF LIEUTENANT JOHN SPRAGGE, WHO DIED OF WOUNDS OFF CAPE SAINT VINCENT . . . A very old cross with the Latin inscription worn away, but he had been told that it once read: TO THE MURDERED VILLAGERS OF DUNSTONHOLME, JUNE 1300 – GOD WILL REPAY. He was almost at the end of the railings, when a tall gaunt figure wearing a clerical collar came out of the lych-gate and blocked his way.

'Ah, there you are, Dr. Allen. I was hoping to catch you. I rather wanted to have a word with you about poor Joe Bates.'

'Of course, Padre, but wouldn't tomorrow do? I am in a bit of a hurry.' About half the village called the Reverend David Ainger 'father', and the rest 'vicar', but Tom used the military compromise. 'I'm meeting Mary at the Crown, you see and . . .' Behind them the clock struck the quarter.

'Oh, I'll not keep you long, my boy, and I'm sure the clientele of the Crown won't let your pretty wife be lonely. It really is important to me that we have a chat.'

'All right, Padre, if you promise it won't be long.' Ainger had a long sallow face which looked as though it had been roughly modelled out of plasticine, but one of the most appealing smiles Tom had ever known. Added to that was an aura which he could only describe as 'goodness'. An impersonal charm that made one want to fit in with his wishes, however irksome they might be. He nodded and followed him across to the vicarage, and into the little gloomy library he called his den.

'Do sit down, Doctor. Oh, excuse me.' The room was littered with books and papers and Ainger removed two heavy volumes from a chair.

'That's better.' He leaned against the fire-place and pulled out his pipe, not lighting it, but fiddling with the bowl.

'I've been to the police station, but they wouldn't let me see Bates, though I did have a few words with Constable Rutter. What I want to ask you is this: do you personally consider that Joe is a lunatic, a cunning murderer, or a person who really did have some sort of supernatural experience?'

'Isn't that a bit of an unfair question, Padre?' Tom tried to settle himself more comfortably in his chair. A loose spring was digging sharply into his thigh. 'After all, I'm just a country G.P., not a detective, a psychiatrist, or a priest. All I can say is what I told the sergeant they sent over from Welcott.'

'And could you repeat that to me, Dr. Allen?' As though suddenly remembering his duties as host, Ainger crossed to a cupboard and poured out two glasses of thick brown liquid. 'I really have a good reason for wanting to know.'

'Of course, I can. There was very little to it. Thank you.' The sherry was sweet and cloying, but Tom sipped at it and told Ainger exactly what he had said to Fenwick. Bates suffered from a weakness of the aorta which could have caused a black-out under severe strain; he had a feeble mentality which, coupled with guilt, might have attributed an act of anger to some divine intervention. Ainger obviously knew all about the way that Bates had been treated over the years by his employer.

As he talked, Tom studied the room. Ainger had been a celebrated mountaineer in his time, and the walls were covered by photographs of roped figures balanced on precipices, or crawling up *arêtes* and dank gullies. A tough old boy, and apparently quite a scholar too. Though he was no theologian himself, he could see that these books were the real thing. Most of the major Greeks bound in leather, Aquinas, Augustine in the Bretain edition, Von Hugel wedged against Spinoza, and not a trace of the popular works which usually take pride of place in Anglican libraries.

The next case appeared to be devoted to a wide range of subjects, and some of them disturbed him slightly. Among *The Golden Bough, Patterns of Culture*, and other standard books on anthropology were dotted: Marshall's *Cult of the Werewolf*, Weber's *Devil in Western Europe*, and a number of medical books. In the top shelf he could see Winter & Reynard's *Teratology . . . A Study of Monstrous Birth*. Its coloured illustrations had given him several sleepless nights when he was a student.

'Thank you, Doctor.' Ainger put down his glass with a sharp click as he finished speaking. 'You preserve a completely open mind, in fact. Colonel Keith provoked Joe Bates just once too often and in the wrong place. He died because Joe was either mentally or physically ill, and that's all there is to it. You haven't thought that his death might be connected with certain other events which have happened in this village?'

'Sorry, but I'm not with you, Padre.' The grandfather clock in the corner showed the half hour. As a doctor's wife, Mary was used to waiting, but this was their day off. 'What other events do you mean?'

'With the salvage ship, perhaps. No, please bear with me a little longer, my boy.' Ainger took a newspaper from his table. 'By all accounts, her master was a most reliable man, yet he suddenly appeared to go mad and charged out to sea through thick fog, destroying himself, his crew, and the crew of that unfortunate tanker which happened to be in his way.

'And today, Joe Bates goes mad too. He'd worked for Keith for years and he must have taken him up Boxer's Hill a hundred times. Why should he suddenly have this stroke or black-out, or whatever it was, and tell a story about feeling that he was being buried alive?

'You've known Joe for some time, Dr. Allen. Do you think he is capable of making it all up?'

'No, and I said so to Sergeant Fenwick.' Tom frowned. 'At the same time, the mind plays queer tricks on one now and again, and he might have imagined it.

'But I can't see any possible connection between him and the *Dalecrest*. Nobody can even guess what happened to her till there has been a full inquiry, and even then . . .' He broke off and shrugged his shoulders.

'Quite right. I don't think we'll know even after the inquiry. Not unless they find survivors, and that appears unlikely now.' Ainger crossed to the window and stared out at the bay, with the sunlight glinting on his spectacles.

'But there have been a lot of unexplained tragedies in this district over the centuries, haven't there? What really happened to the Children of Paul? Why should a group of normally peaceful people suddenly turn into vicious murderers?'

'I haven't the slightest idea, Padre. After all, it happened several hundred years ago.' Tom struggled to conceal his irritation. He was fond of Ainger, but the old boy really did appear to be getting very strange.

The Children of Paul were members of a religious cult led by a monk named Paul of Ely. Like many other medieval sects, they believed themselves to be contaminated by the rest of humanity, and decided to withdraw from the world. The story went that they arrived in Dunstonholme in 1300 on their way to one of the Feyne Islands where they hoped to found their community. Being refused transport by the Franklin, they killed the villagers and the small garrison of the castle, and set out in stolen boats which promptly capsized and drowned all of them. There was some factual evidence, Tom supposed, but most of it was just legend, like Arthur, and Robin Hood, and Gog-Magog.

'Yes, six hundred and sixty-six years ago, almost to a day, but there have been more recent events as well.' Ainger's voice droned on against the tick of the clock. 'Do you know why we have no railway here? They started a line from Welcott, but it was never finished. When they got as far as the moors, the navvies refused to work on the cutting.

'Then there was the lead mine up near Salter's Gate. Lord Mayne financed it to ease local unemployment in 1880, but it closed down after only a few weeks, because nobody would work there. They said there was a curse on the place.'

'I thought the shaft was supposed to be unsafe because of loose rock.' How old was Ainger, Tom wondered? At least seventy-five, and his mind appeared to be running down fast. There were no relatives either. They'd have to see about finding him a living-in housekeeper if he got any worse.

'Yes, that was the official reason they gave for the closure, but no local people believed it. There are more things though; so many more.' Ainger turned from the window and stared at a tarnished silver crucifix on the far wall. Behind his glasses, the eyes didn't look as though they were focusing correctly.

'The night the American ship was bombed, for instance. That terrible business at Pounder's Hole. You probably think I'm mad, Doctor, and in a way I hope you are right. But, I honestly believe that all these events are connected, and there is something hellish surrounding this village. A dreadful danger which is going to break out very soon.'

'I don't think you're mad, Padre. I do think that Keith's death has upset you, however, and I'd like you to come and see me in the morning.' Tom stood up and held out his hand. 'I must go now, I'm afraid.'

'Yes, yes, of course. It is very kind of you to have spared me so much time.' The parson's hand was hard and muscular, but there was no grip in it.

'You get along, my boy, and don't worry about me. Just give my love to your wife and say I'm sorry I delayed you. You can find your own way out?'

'Of course. Now, take a couple of those pills I gave you last week and get a good night's sleep.' Tom didn't like leaving him in such a state. He opened the door and then paused as Ainger called him back.

'Dr. Allen, I know you must think I'm insane, and, as I said before, I almost hope you are right. There is a way of proving it though.' There was a ring of authority in his voice.

'When you get to the Crown, do something for me. Go up to Frank Jessop and ask him what he did on the night of the bombing.'

CHAPTER FOUR

'Don't give it another thought, Doc. Your missus and I have been having a capital time in your absence.' Mr. Moldon Mott gave Mary a proprietorial smirk which Tom found quite revolting. He had a big gingery face, a gingery moustache and his body looked as though it weighed about sixteen stone, almost all of it bone and muscle. 'Haven't we, my dear?'

'It's been great fun.' To Tom's further annoyance, Mary looked as though she meant it. 'Mr. Mott has been telling about a new restaurant that's just opened in Tynecastle. We thought we might all go there together.'

'If you've no objection of course, Doc.' The saloon bar of the Crown was unusually empty, probably on account of Keith's death, and Mott's rich booming voice seemed to fill the whole room.

'No, of course not.' Tom had every possible objection, but he could hardly say so. He was worried about Bates, he was worried about Ainger, and he had been looking forward to having a quiet meal with Mary. He resented Mott's presence and he also resented being called 'Doc'.

'Good, that's settled then. It's an East-Indian place called the Java Head. I spent some time in those parts, so I know what to order. One local delicacy I remember was chopped goat's udder stewed in its own milk and garnished with green peppers. Quite delicious.

'I suggest we have another couple of noggins here, and then push on. You'll be interested to see what my bus can do on a decent road.' Mott grinned through the window at an enormous American vehicle covered with fins and badges and batteries of head lamps that practically filled the car park. It made the Allens' elderly Rover look like the small survivor of a distant age.

'Charlie, let's have some service.' He snapped his fingers and the aged waiter at the counter almost jumped to attention and hurried towards them, increasing Tom's irritation still more. Usually Charlie was the reverse of obliging, but like the rest of the village, he appeared to have fallen under Mott's spell.

The fellow was a bit of a personage, of course. Explorer and man of letters was the way he described himself, and there was an imposing array of volumes in the local library to prove it: *Mott's Wanderings in Central America*, *With Mott Across the Lost Kalahari* and *The Hidden Treasures of the Amazon by J. Moldon Mott* were a few of the titles. Tom had also heard that certain of the world's geographical features bore his name: the Mott River which ran into Hudson's Bay, Mount Moldon Mott in South Africa, and Mott's Leap somewhere up in the highlands of Scotland. At the same time there was no need for Charlie to grovel in front of him.

'The same for Mrs. Allen and myself, Charlie. And what's your poison?' Mott's eyebrows came up in a bar as Tom ordered beer.

'You should watch that, you know. You're a young man, but there's the trace of a pot already.' A gnarled finger poked Tom in the stomach. 'Still, Doctor knows best, eh, though it could be a case of "physician heal thyself" before long. Now I haven't got an ounce of surplus flesh on me.'

'No, I suppose not.' Tom looked coldly away. Solly Black had taken his wrongs to the public bar, and he could hear the list of losses being recited across the counter. 'Five standard cats – that's two and a half quid; three de-luxe cats with ribbons – thirty bob each, they are; six . . .'

'But you were going to tell us about the vicar, darling.' Mary leaned forward. She was a small fair girl with a surprisingly mobile face which could change its expression in seconds. A moment ago she had been smiling at Mott's sallies, but now she looked deeply concerned. 'Is he really ill, do you think?'

'No, not exactly ill, but he's starting to run down. Probably his heart isn't getting enough blood to the brain. Also, living alone as he does, with only a daily woman, can't help. He was certainly talking very oddly this evening, and I wouldn't be surprised if he wasn't developing a persecution complex. I'd like to get him to see a specialist, but I doubt if he'll agree.'

'Ah, thanks, Charlie.' Mott beamed up at the waiter. 'It looks as if you've managed to get the right amount of Angostura this time, so you can keep the change. Cheers to both of you.' He raised his glass and clicked it against Mary's.

'As it happens, I bumped into old Ainger myself about a couple of hours ago. He's certainly eccentric, but I wouldn't call him senile – not by a long chalk. He told me that ever since he came to Dunstonholme, over thirty years ago, he's had sudden premonitions of danger – of evil hanging over the village. He appeared to be about to tell me what he thought caused them, and then suddenly broke off, as though he were ashamed to.'

'Yes, he's odd enough, but there's nothing mad about such premonitions. I've had them myself many times. Once in East Africa, for instance . . .' Mott launched into a long and boastful account of a meeting with a rhinoceros.

'But what did Ainger actually say to you, Doc?' The rhino had been finally dispatched with great brutality and Mott took another swig of pink gin. 'Did he ask you if you felt there was a connection between Keith's death and the loss of the salvage ship?'

'That among other things.' Tom was becoming tired of the subject, but at least it gave him an excuse to hear his own voice instead of Mott's for a while. He repeated everything that Ainger had said. The Children of Paul – the railway line which was never completed – the lead mine that closed down – something that happened at a place called Pounder's Hole – something that Frank Jessop had done on the night of the bombing.

'Yes, that's more or less what he said to me.' Mott passed across his cigarette case. 'A number of unexplained events which are all

somehow connected running back through the centuries. Thanks.'
He leaned towards Tom's lighter.

'Though he wouldn't tell me what he thought caused them, he
did say that there is something in this area which resents outsid-
ers, and all these events were manifestations of it. Those chaps,
the Children of Paul, were intending to settle on a near-by island,
and they were driven mad. The railway would have opened up the
district, so it was stopped. The lead mine might have brought in an
outside labour force: it closed down.

'No, you're probably right, I suppose. It sounds quite ridiculous
when one repeats it. The poor old blighter may very well have a
screw loose.' Mott frowned as he dragged on the cigarette.

'All the same, there is something a bit odd about this village. I
sensed it myself after a few days. It's rather like the atmosphere
you get in certain houses. They may be crumbling ruins or bright
modern villas, but there's a feeling that you can cut with a knife
of being unwelcome in them. As you know, I came here to write
a book, but though I'm usually a fast worker I haven't finished a
chapter in over a fortnight. Every time I sit down at the typewriter,
something seems to be trying to stop me.'

'I've had that too.' Mary nodded. 'When I've been walking on
the moors sometimes, I've had the sensation of being watched.
As though there was something always behind me that bitterly
resented my being there.'

'Have you, my dear? How very unpleasant.' Mott smiled sympa-
thetically, but he obviously preferred Mary in the role of a listener.

'Ainger didn't mention anything to me about Frank Jessop, or
Pounder's Hole. That name would make a nice title for a juvenile
mystery, by the way – The Adventure of Pounder's Hole or The Twins
Find Treasure at Pounder's Hole.'

'What is it, a cave?'

'Yes, it's up on the moors about four miles to the north. I've
never been there, or heard much about it, but we've only lived in
Dunstonholme for three years, and the locals are a pretty reticent
lot.'

'I have though, Tom.' Mary put down her glass sharply. 'Don't
you remember Mrs. Shaftoe? She was a char we had when we first

came here, Mr. Mott. A very nice woman, but she used to bring a terrible son of six with her who made far more mess than his mother cleared up.

'One day, however, and it was the only time I can remember, Billy was a model of good behaviour. Instead of charging about the house, he stood quietly in the kitchen reading a comic for the whole morning. I asked if he was ill and she grinned at me.

' "Oh, yes, 'e's ill in a way, Missus. 'E's sore." ' Mary's voice was as flexible as her face, and Tom could distinctly hear Mrs. Shaftoe speaking.

' " 'E told me that 'im and some of 'is young friends were going a' blackberrying up at that darned Pounder's Hole. I didn't 'arf lace his arse for 'im. It's not canny that place, Missus, and everybody in the village knows it." '

'Did she indeed? How very interesting. Mrs. Shaftoe appears to have been a woman of strong arm and character.' Mott looked down at his empty glass. 'What about a final refill for the road?'

'Yes, of course.' Tom beckoned to the waiter, who came across much more slowly this time and addressed himself to Mott, though it was clearly Tom's turn.

'The same again, sir?'

'No, I'll have a double this time, Charlie. And I think that Dr. Allen would like you to have one yourself. A drop of brandy goes down very well, I've heard.'

'Yes, indeed, sir. I'm very partial to a glass of Martell. Thank you, Mr. Mott. And you too of course, Dr. Allen.' There was an almost boyish spring in the old man's step as he hurried to the counter.

'Noah, I didn't see 'um, not at the beginning, but I heard the bastard.' Solly Black appeared to have left, and a thick beery voice was dominating the public bar. Tom recognized it as belonging to Frank Jessop, the owner of Blyegate Farm.

'My dawg here, Lady Jane, spotted 'um first, of course. Grand little bitch Jane. One of the real old border breed, out of Candy Floss by Mosstrooper. She took second prize at the Otterford Trials last year, as you know, with the Queen Mother there t' hand me ther cup.' Though not one of the village's most sober citizens, Mr.

Jessop worked his farm single-handed, and was greatly respected on account of his wonderful way with animals.

'Leanin' against the wall, I was, 'aving a bit of a breather after muckin' out th' cow byre, when I hears this screeching noise and Jane goes through the gate like th' Devil was arter 'er. I looks round, and old Keith shoots past in his chair, yellin' 'is bloody head off. I thought I'd burst me sides laughin'.' A fist crashed on the counter to drive home the point, and Tom remembered that a few months previously Jessop had been heavily fined for being drunk in charge of an agricultural tractor, following a complaint by Colonel Keith.

'Yus, down 'e went, with Jane and them Baker kids running arter 'um, and my old shorthorn bull, Rusty, blaring away in the paddock to give 'um a send-off. I know animals aren't supposed to think, but old Rusty sounded as pleased as I was to see the back of th' bastard. 'E knows that Keith shopped me all right. More like a brother than a bull, Rusty is to me.'

'So, that's Mr. Jessop, is it? The chap who did something on the night of the bombing.' Mott glanced at his watch. Outside the sun was going down and long shadows were creeping across the village. 'We might have a word with him before we leave.

'Ah, there you are, Charlie.' Mott beamed up at the waiter, like an emperor complimenting one of his bodyguard on some major feat of bravery.

'Yes, here we are, sir. A dry sherry for Madam, a bitter for you, Doctor, and your large pink gin, Mr. Mott. I mixed it myself, so it should be just right.' There was a brandy glass on the tray and Charlie raised it ceremoniously.

'And I'd like to say that I hope your stay here will be long and profitable, Mr. Mott. Your very good health, sir.' He knocked back the brandy in a single quick movement. 'That will be twelve and sixpence please, Dr. Allen.

'Thank you, sir. I got a couple of your books out of the library last week, Mr. Mott, and I've been reading the African one to my grandson. Though he's only six, he's thoroughly enjoying himself. Laughed and laughed he did over that bit where you flogged all those game poachers.'

'Did he indeed?' There was a pleased smile on Mott's face. 'He sounds an intelligent little boy.'

'Now, tell me something, Charlie. A few miles to the north of here, there's a cave called Pounder's Hole. Why is it that nobody from the village goes there?'

'Oh that, sir.' The man's face became slightly paternal. 'You were talking to the vicar this evening, weren't you, Mr. Mott? Very interested in local history, Father Ainger is. A very highly educated gentleman indeed. But, though maybe I shouldn't say so in front of Dr. Allen, perhaps he's a little past it nowadays. A little . . .' He raised a finger and tapped his forehead.

'No, there's nothing in that story about Pounder's Hole. All the moor around there is full of bogs and pitfalls, and the rocks are loose and dangerous. That's the only reason we keep away from it. Even those pot-holers, as they call themselves, don't go up there. A few years ago, just before you came to Dunstonholme, Doctor, an R.A.F. pilot made a forced landing on the moor. He brought the plane down perfectly, but they never found his body. It appears that he must have wandered off for help and fallen down some shaft. After that, the Church Commissioners who own the land had it fenced off to keep animals out.'

'But what is the story, Charlie?'

'Well, it's just a sort of legend, Madam. A fairy tale to frighten the children away, you might say. Over a hundred years ago, it was supposed to have happened. This chap, Pounder, was a recluse, and he planned to build himself a cottage up there, quarrying the stone locally. They found his body almost crushed into the earth one day. I think he must have been caught by a rock fall.'

'Yes, that's all very well, Charlie, but there's more to it, isn't there? You say that you think he was caught by a fall of rock. But what did your parents say?'

'Oh, it was all so silly, Mr. Mott, that I hardly like to repeat it. I believed it when I was a lad, of course, but . . .' He shook his head at youthful credence. 'The old people used to tell us to stay away from the place because there was something up there that drove men and animals mad. They said that Pounder had been trampled to death by a flock of sheep.'

'Yes, it's ridiculous, isn't it, Doctor? I know that some of those big tups – that's our local name for a ram, Mr. Mott – can be a bit rough at times, but these were supposed to be ordinary grazing ewes. Just a tale to keep the kids away. And now, if you will excuse me please, I really must be going.' A couple at another table were beckoning for service and he crossed over to them.

'And we had better be going too, if we want a meal.' Tom finished his beer and stood up. 'I must say that I've had my fill of local folklore for one day. Trampled to death by sheep indeed!'

'Yes, I agree. It does sound very unlikely.' Mott helped Mary on with her coat. 'Excuse me for just one second, though. I'd rather like to hear about the last thing that Ainger said to you.' He sauntered over to the counter.

'Good evening, Mr. Jessop,' he said, smiling pleasantly across into the public bar. 'I wonder if I might have the pleasure of buying you a drink?'

'Well, that's very civil of you, sir.' The farmer grinned at his almost full tankard. 'I've still got a drop in 'ere, but another wouldn't do me any harm at all. Brown ale it is, Mr. Mott.'

'Excellent.' Mott's smile widened and he nodded to the barman. 'I'm afraid I can't stay to join you, but I wonder if you would tell me something, Mr. Jessop? What exactly was it that you did on the night of the bombing?' His smile went out and he leapt sideways as Jessop, his face contorted, picked up the tankard and flung it straight at Mott's head.

CHAPTER FIVE

'Damn yer! Damn yer to hell.' Frank Jessop shouted at the top of his voice as he half ran, half staggered down the street. Since being ejected from the Crown he had visited two other public houses in the village and he was very drunk indeed.

'I'll kill yer, just see if I don't.' He collided with a pillar-box, and stood staring stupidly at it. His left eye was almost closed now, and becoming very painful, but it wasn't Mott he wanted to kill. Mott had asked the question. Mott had vaulted over the counter after he threw the glass, and blacked his eye before the barmen pulled them apart. Mott was a bastard, but he had had his revenge on him when the dog, Jane, tore open his trousers. It was Ainger he was after.

'Yer promised. Yer gave me a solemn promise, that yer'd never tell a soul about it.' His words died to a mutter as he considered the enormity of Ainger's offence.

'Yer said it was our secret, and would never go any further. And now, twenty-three years later, yer bring it out.' His hands twisted together as though they were already round the vicar's neck, crushing the life out of him.

'Yes, I'll kill yer, yer bastard.' Windows were opening, and people were watching him from the opposite pavement, but though the moon was bright, Jessop didn't see them. All he could see was Ainger's face and hear his Judas voice. 'Don't worry, Mr. Jessop. Nobody will ever know what happened, and I shall regard the whole matter as though we had been in the confessional together.' He turned away from the pillar-box and stumbled on.

'All right, Frank, that's quite enough of that.' He was fifty yards from the vicarage gate when the bulky form of Constable Rutter appeared before him.

'Just you behave yourself, lad. We've been friends for a long time, and I've had a hard day with old Keith's death. Don't you go making more trouble for me.

'Oh, no you don't.' He caught Jessop's arm as he tried to push past him. 'If that gentleman you threw the glass at had wanted to prefer charges, you'd be in the cell right now, so just count yourself lucky. Besides, I've been looking for you about another matter. You'd better get back up to the farm and see to that old bull of yours.'

'My bull? Rusty?' The image of Ainger's face growing black above his fingers slowly faded. 'What's the matter with him, Ken?'

'That I don't know, Frank, but I was at the bottom of the lane a while back, and I could hear him blaring his head off. Sounded as if he were in pain. Could he have caught himself on some wire?'

'Noah, ther ain't no wire in the paddock.' Jessop shook his head. 'The old fool must have been eating that blasted poison ivy again. I keep tearing it out – burning it, but it always creeps back. Probably he's swole up.'

'Well, whatever it is, you'd best cut along back to him, Frank.'

'Yes, yes, I'll go, but I gotter see Ainger first. I must see 'um, Ken.'

'You'll see the vicar in the morning, when you're sober, but right now you've got a sick animal to look after. I always heard you were fond of that bull, Frank.'

'Fond of 'um. Course I'm fond of 'um.' Jessop pulled his arm free. 'Reared Rusty by hand I did. Gentle as a kitten he is with me. Yes, you're right, Ken, I'd best go and see to 'um. But don't think I won't settle with that bastard, Ainger, in the morning.' He turned and lurched back up the street with the dog at a regulation three paces from his heels.

Damn Ainger, though, he thought. Why did he have to go and break his promise after all these years? Twenty-three years and he'd sworn that he'd never tell a soul. As he reached the bottom of the lane, Jessop looked up at the sky. It had been a night just like this when it happened. A motorist had told him that one of his sheep was lying injured by the burn, and he had gone out to her. The moon had been almost full, as it was tonight, and the ridges of the moors appeared to stretch endlessly away to the north. There were no lights in the village of course, but Tynecastle was copping it, and he could see a flicker of gun-fire in the sky, and now and then the sudden glare of a bomb.

All was quiet at Dunstonholme, though, and that had made him feel strangely guilty. Two months previously his brother had joined the navy, and how he envied him. Somebody had to keep the farm going of course, work of national importance; but he had felt inadequate and rejected, as though he were somehow inferior to other men. What happened later that night proved it to be true. That was why he had never married, why he drank so much, why he relied on the company of animals who didn't ask questions. Before the year was out Bill had been frozen to death in a lifeboat, but he still envied him.

Yes, twenty-three bloody years ago. As he toiled up the hill, Jessop forced himself to remember exactly how it had been. The same swollen white moon, the black ridges of the fells, and the flicker of the barrage in the south. Where the lane turned and ran along the cliffs, he had looked down and seen the ships at anchor in the bay: four small coasters and a big American freighter waiting to join a convoy, with their grey paint looking like silver in the moonlight. Somehow, the sight of them increased his feeling of inadequacy.

The sheep was there all right. Old Jessie, one of his best ewes, lying beside the burn with a hind leg broken in two places, and there was only one thing he could do.

'Sorry, Jessie,' he had said, pillowing the frightened head against his chest as he drew out the knife. 'Sorry, old girl.' For a few seconds the blood pulsed from the severed artery and then the eyes glazed. He had pushed her away from him and knelt down beside the stream to wash his hands. As he did so he saw the plane.

It looked small and completely harmless at first: a tiny black cross circling like a hawk in the moonlight and drifting silently down. The pilot had obviously cut his engines in the hope of making a surprise attack. Jessop watched fascinated, expecting that at any moment one of the look-outs on the ships would see her and the guns start to fire.

But nothing happened. The bomber just drifted slowly on till it was barely a hundred feet above the water. He began to wonder if it was out of control, and then the American ship was suddenly hidden by a gout of purple flame, and seconds later the hills echoed with the explosion.

And then the plane came for him. The engines had burst into life again, and she roared up to the lip of the cliff in a bouncing arc, straight towards the place where he was kneeling. As it did so, Jessop knew terror. His head seemed to be about to burst and the water appeared to be boiling around his hands, but he couldn't move them. He just stared at that hurtling black shape, knowing that in a second the guns would open up or a bomb plough him into the ground. It came so close that he could see the bomb-aimer's face peering down at him, and then it swung over the hillside and turned out to sea.

The bomber had gone, and he was alone on the moor. He was

quite safe, and there was nobody near him. So, why was he still screaming? Why was sweat pouring from his forehead into the boiling water, and why had the moon vanished? With a sudden convulsive effort, he had pulled himself to his feet and stood swaying in the pitch darkness.

For though the plane had gone, another danger had taken its place. A far worse danger. He had sensed it all around him. Something which was obscene and rotten and incredibly old. A thing with the power to turn off the moon like a lamp and hide the glare of the burning ship. A thing which could destroy his body as well as his soul. He had heard it coming too. A heavy thudding noise in his head like the beat of a worn-out machine. He had put his hands to his ears and run blindly down the lane till he slipped and lay sobbing on the gravel. He was still lying there when David Ainger, driving home from an A.R.P. meeting at Welcott, found him two hours later.

But why? Why had Ainger talked about it after all these years? With the clean air on his face and the exertion of climbing the hill, Jessop was sobering up and he felt more bewilderment than anger.

Ainger had been so kind at the time. He had helped him into his car, told him that it was merely shock, brought about by seeing the plane hurtle over him, and promised never to mention what had happened to anybody. Why did he suddenly go and break his promise now?

There was Rusty, though. A long mournful bellow which could have been caused by either rage or extreme pain rang out across the moor. Ken Rutter hadn't made up the story to get him to go home peacefully, then. Why couldn't the fool leave that bloody ivy alone? He'd been swollen up with it twice before. Surely he should have learned his lesson by now?

Jessop hurried on and then frowned slightly as the road turned. He'd lived on Boxer's Hill all his life, and he knew it much better than he did the back of his hand, but tonight it looked different. The moors were just the same of course, the bay was spread out to his right, and at the next bend he would see his farm. Something was missing though, and after a few seconds he realized what it was. Usually, at this time of night, there were sheep grazing by the roadside, but now there wasn't one within a mile of him, though he could see them up on the fell like a clump of white mushrooms in the moonlight.

That was strange. He paused for a moment, and turned up his coat collar. Something else was different too. When he stopped, Jane always came forward and leaned against his legs. He'd trained her to do that, so she'd stay by him during his frequent visits to the Crown. He looked back and frowned again. The dog was far away down the lane, with her body crouched low in an attitude of complete dejection.

'Come on, girl. Come on, Jane,' he shouted. 'You're surely not frightened of old Rusty, are you? Come to me, girl.' Damn the fool! What was the matter with her? He was about to go back to her when the noise ahead increased to pandemonium.

There were more than Rusty making all that racket. He could hear the cows in the byre bellowing too, and a shrill cackle of poultry.

So, that was it. Jessop grunted with relief. Some damned fox had got in among the hens and the animals were helping to give the warning. Rusty was all right, though he would have to do something about that ivy all the same. Decent of Ken Rutter to tell him, and he'd better hurry, if he didn't want to lose all his hens. He broke into a run, and then stopped as he heard a crash of timber and an enormous shape appeared at the bend before him.

'Rusty, yer are a blamed idiot. Scared of a little fox, are yer, lad?' The bull looked oddly dejected, but its right fore foot pounded the surface of the lane.

'So, you smashed down the fence, yer old devil. It'll be barbed wire for you from now on.' The huge foot still beat on the gravel, but Jessop knew no fear. He'd reared the animal by hand, and where he was concerned it was as gentle as a kitten. They understood each other like brothers, and in spite of the vet's protests, he'd never even ringed its nose.

'All right, Rusty. Come to me and we'll go home together. Come to me, lad.' The foot stopped pounding, and his voice suddenly rose to a scream. 'For the love of God, Rusty.'

Frank Jessop was a badly educated man and he would never

have appreciated the irony of using Colonel Keith's last words. He just stood there screaming them, as the bull lowered its head and charged.

CHAPTER SIX

'Well, what about it? Do you think it could be the catamaran this time?' Captain Saxby of Her Majesty's frigate *Dunbar* stared at the tiny white dot on the radar screen. 'About the right size, isn't it?'

'Near enough, sir, but one can't be sure of anything at this range.' The operator made a slight adjustment to his set. 'She appears to be circling, though. My guess is that it's just another fishing boat, sir.'

'I see. Then let's hope your guess is wrong, Healey. Course green four zero, quartermaster.' Saxby nodded pleasantly, but he was getting increasingly tired of false alarms – there had been three of them in the last hour: a Russian trawler, a Grimsby drifter and an unidentified object which had suddenly vanished, probably a whale. He glanced at the wheel-house clock, as *Dunbar* swung to port at her full thirty-five knots. They had been ordered to search till midnight and there were less than twenty minutes to go.

'If it is the *Tinker-Taylor*, sir, and they are trying to make Russia, she's miles off course.' His first lieutenant was bent over the chart table. 'We know that neither of them has any knowledge of navigation, but even allowing for that, they should be much farther north by now.'

'We can't allow for anything, Number One. Is she still circling, Healey?' As he looked at the screen he considered the catamaran's specifications: thirty foot, sixty horse-power outboards on each hull, with flexible feeds to a central fuel tank that gave her a maximum range of fourteen hours. The tank hadn't been full when she was stolen and, even in this calm sea and at the most economical cruising speed, they couldn't be using the engines much longer. With enormous luck, they might manage to sail her round the North Cape, but personally he doubted it. His own guess, from what he had heard about Rails and Dander, was that they would try to reach Norway and steal more fuel there. They had got away with so much already that they might well imagine they had some sort of divine protection.

Yes, Rails and Dander. Saxby smiled to himself. Two very bright boys indeed. In a way he almost hoped that they did get away with it. Anti-social, of course, but what a terrible waste to put them in prison. Both under nineteen, but they had broken out, robbed a mail van, and finally made off with this *Tinker-Taylor*. Officer material with great prospects, if they could be moulded in the right way. He wished he had a few like them in *Dunbar*'s wardroom.

Tinker-Taylor – what a ridiculous name for a boat. He looked with distaste at the three civilians in the corner of the wheel-house: her owner, Mrs. Maxwell Randersen, a police inspector named Jones who had been violently sick the moment they left Tyneport, and a stolid sergeant whose name he hadn't caught. He had hoped they would remain below, but Mrs. Randersen had pleaded to be up on the bridge, and her husband was not only a millionaire, but a close friend of the Second Sea Lord. She'd wanted to bring a lap dog with her too, but he'd put his foot down there.

Damn the woman! Her yachting cap and jacket had enough gold braid to fit out an admiral, and the skintight slacks were plainly indecent for one of her age and bulk. Why couldn't she have seen that there was a watchman on board her blasted boat? The *Dunbar* had been due for leave today, and he bitterly resented its postponement.

'Target in sight, sir. Dead ahead. Range eight thousand yards.' The midshipman by the telephones repeated the message from the crow's nest. 'It appears to be circling to starboard, sir.'

'Thank you.' Another trawler then. Saxby's feelings were a mixture of frustration and relief. He was sick of the false alarms, but part of him wished it wouldn't be *Dunbar* that returned Rails and Dander to their cells. The next report dashed that hope. 'Yes, it's the catamaran, sir. Still circling to starboard.'

'I see.' Saxby stepped out on to the wing of the flying bridge, and lifted his binoculars. In the bright moonlight there was no need for night-glasses. Yes, that was the *Tinker-Taylor* all right. She was swinging round in tight circles, and he guessed what had probably happened: the boys had put her on automatic pilot and turned in for a few hours. While they were sleeping one of the engines must have cut out.

'My congratulations, Captain. You've got the young devils, then.' Inspector Jones lumbered unsteadily to his side. 'A very smart piece of work, if I may say so.'

'Thank you.' Saxby lowered the glasses. 'And what happens if they don't give up quietly, but decide to make a fight for it? From what Mrs. Randersen told us, they appear to be pretty well armed.' Among the catamaran's inventory was a shot gun, two sporting rifles, and a Colt automatic. There were permits for them, of course. Men like Maxwell Randersen had permits for everything. 'I'm not going to put a shell through her, if that's what you expect.'

'Oh no, sir. That won't be necessary.' Jones had obviously recovered from his attack of sea sickness, and he grinned hugely. 'I don't think the Press would be very kind to us if we did that, and I'm sure Mrs. Randersen wouldn't like us to damage her pretty little ship.' The Dunbar was closing in rapidly and the yacht was clear in the moonlight. There was no sign of life on her deck.

'If you could just stop her, and wake the lads up at the same time, I'll do all the rest, sir.'

'Very well.' Saxby turned to a midshipman. 'Ask Guns to knock out that engine for me, Mr. Macdonald. Tell him not to use tracers, of course. I don't want the fuel tank going up.' He was about to turn to the quartermaster, but saw there was no need. The first lieutenant had already given the order and Dunbar was turning to starboard and following the catamaran's wake. A second later there was a short burst of machine-gun fire, the outboard stopped, and the Tinker-Taylor drifted for a few yards and then lay pitching on the slight swell.

'Thank you very much, sir.' Jones lurched against him as the engines were thrown into reverse to bring Dunbar to a shuddering halt. 'You've got a good marksman there, it seems. And now, if I might have the use of your speaking device for a moment, we'll soon have the young blighters back where they belong. Thank you, my boy.' He took a microphone from the midshipman.

'All right, you two. We know you're there, so let's have no more fun and games. Just come out on deck with your hands over your heads.' Jones's voice was pleasant, almost fatherly, and Saxby began to revise his earlier opinion of him.

'Come on, Rails. Come on, Mr. Dander. This is Inspector Jones talking, and I don't like being kept waiting.' The loud hailer was at full power and the two vessels were less than fifty yards apart, but there was still no sign of life on the catamaran. 'You've had a good run for your money, boys, but it's all over now, and you haven't got a chance.'

'They're not going to play ball, then?' Though he would never have admitted it, Saxby felt slightly pleased.

'Maybe not, sir.' The inspector switched off the microphone. 'I don't understand it, though. Neither of them are fools, and they must realize that the game's up. If it becomes necessary, could you shoot a line on to the yacht and pull her alongside?'

'We can do that for you,' Saxby nodded.

'Good.' Jones lifted the microphone again and there was a sudden anger in his voice.

'Now, listen to me, you two. I'm giving you just three minutes to come out on deck, and after that you'll be in for it. If you want trouble there's a four-inch gun pointing at you, and we won't hesitate to use it.

'Should either of you survive, which I doubt, there'll be no comfortable time at a Borstal for you, but a damn long spell of preventive detention in a tough prison.

'Right, you have exactly three minutes from . . . now.' He consulted his watch and replaced the microphone.

'That should bring the blighters out, Captain Saxby, unless . . . Yes, unless they're tight.' He turned to Mrs. Randersen.

'Is there anything to drink on your boat, Madam?'

'But of course there is, Inspector.' She had an over-genteel accent which struggled to conceal a trace of Birmingham. 'We have a marvellous cocktail bar that Maxwell stocked himself. You name the poison, and we've got it.' She gave a little tinkling laugh and then frowned suddenly.

'But you surely don't mean what you said, Inspector, about

shelling the *Tinker-Taylor*? She cost over twenty thousand pounds, you know, and I've only had her three months.'

'No, there won't be any need for that, Madam. Those lads wouldn't have ignored your bar, and my guess is that they'll be as tight as ticks. Out for the count, both of 'em.' Once again he lifted the microphone. 'All right, Rails and Dander. You've got a minute and a half, and that's the last warning you'll have from me.' He looked at Saxby and frowned.

'Yes, sir. They must be drunk, or waiting for the last moment to come out. All the same, there's no sense in our playing heroes, and we'd best take a few precautions. If you have to pull them alongside of us, I'd like as few people on deck as possible. Neither of them are supposed to be violent boys, but one never knows.'

'Very well.' Saxby gave an order to the midshipman. 'Now, what about an armed party to go aboard?'

'Oh no, sir. There won't be any need for that. Me and Sergeant Collarbone can handle everything. But, I think the time's up now.' He watched admiringly as Saxby raised his hand. A rocket shot across the water, caught the catamaran's stern rail, and a line tightened.

'Wonderful, Captain. Really wonderful, these modern inventions. You ready, Harry?'

'Ready as I'll ever be, Inspector.' They were the first words Saxby had heard the sergeant utter since he came on board.

'Good lad.' The *Tinker-Taylor* came alongside the frigate with hardly a sound, and Jones grinned at Saxby again. 'Yes, a really wonderful contrivance that.

'Well, we'll be on our way, sir. If they are out cold, I'd be glad of a couple of chaps with stretchers later on. My feet are none too steady, I'm afraid.' As though to prove the point, Jones lurched clumsily to the ladder and lowered himself down.

No, those two aren't dangerous, he thought, as he crossed the deck. Rails: shop breaking, a couple of smash and grabs, and the forgery of a Post Office savings book. Dander: blackmail and living on immoral earnings. Nice record for a couple of eighteen-year-old boys, but no history of violence between them. All the same, one could never be sure. The feel of the heavy revolver in his shoulder holster was great comfort, as was the knowledge that Collarbone had once won a cup at Bisley.

It would be all right though. They must be drunk not to have heard that. The catamaran moved much more than the *Dunbar*, and he landed on her deck with a crash. The poor little devils must have known the game was up when the starboard engine gave out, and decided to have a last fling. He didn't blame them, but he'd see they got a good long stretch added to their sentences all the same.

'Right, Sergeant. You cover me, and shoot to kill, if there's any trouble. No messing about with flesh wounds.' He raised his voice in case they were capable of hearing him, and moved forward to the cabin door. There was a light behind it, and he felt his heart-beats quicken as he grasped the handle. They weren't thought to be violent, but there were two rifles, a shotgun and a .45 automatic aboard. This could be the last action of his life. He pulled back the door and gasped with relief.

'Yes, you're right, Inspector. Stewed to the gills, the pair of 'em.' Collarbone grinned, as he followed him across the fiddley. 'Blimey! It's like a ruddy whore's boudoir.'

'You can say that again, Harry.' Jones's eyes swept around the cabin. Mrs. Randersen had exotic tastes, to say the least, and it did look more like a room in a brothel than part of a ship: gilded chairs, mirrored walls, a glittering cocktail cabinet, and two huge divan beds upholstered in scarlet plush. Rails lay on one of them, and Dander on the other. The poor sods really had been knocking it back and they were both unconscious.

'Right, lad. It's time to get up now. Wakey-wakey, Billy.' He took hold of Dander's shoulder, and then drew back shuddering, as the face tilted sideways into the light. Billy Dander had two mouths. One of them was tightly closed and in the place where it should have been, but the other had no right to be there, and made him look as though he were screaming at the top of his voice: a jagged, four-inch gash, wide open beneath the chin.

'Jesus Ker-ist.' Collarbone's voice was almost a sob. 'Come and look over here, Inspector. It's like an animal had done it.' He had turned Rails on to his back to show a criss-cross of wounds running from the neck to the waist. 'A ruddy animal.'

'Don't be a fool, Harry.' Jones looked at the deck and saw a carving knife lying beside the cocktail cabinet. 'It's obvious enough what happened. They fell out over something when they were tight and did each other in.' Even as he spoke, he knew that was impossible. The wounds ruled it out, as did the position of the bodies. Somebody else had been with them when they stole the boat. Somebody else was on board now. At the end of the cabin, there was another door swinging open and he moved towards it.

'Cover me again, Harry,' he said, transferring his own gun back to his right hand, and pulled back the door.

The bathroom was as exotic as the cabin: a lavatory pan supported by a plunging dolphin, a smiling nymph holding the wash basin, and a shower cabinet of black and green marble. Mrs. Randersen had been washing her smalls before the theft and they hung from a pipe against the bulkhead: frilly black knickers, a black slip, an extraordinary thing of nylon and elastic, and a black stocking.

Just one stocking, because its partner was in use. Inside the shower cabinet, a man's body was swinging. Sea water still dripped from his clothes, and his face was so contorted that it hardly looked human.

'And just who is he?' Jones reached out into the breast pocket and drew out a seaman's discharge book. It was soaking wet and the pages were stuck together. The ink had run too, and he had to put on his glasses to read it.

'All right, Harry. Get back to the frigate and tell them to radio the shore. Say that we've found Rails and Dander and also . . .' He frowned as he pushed the book into his pocket. 'Also, John Daniels, bos'n of that salvage ship which blew up the other day.'

CHAPTER SEVEN

'No, Mr. Mott, I'm very sorry, but I can't tell you anything.' Though the vicarage was only a few hundred yards away, Ainger's voice on the telephone was so faint that he might have been speaking over long distance. 'I can't break a promise to an old friend.'

'But Jessop is dead, Vicar.' With the telephone pressed against his ear and a deep scowl on his face, Mott resembled a caricature of Rodin's 'Thinker'. 'Surely that releases you from your promise?'

'No, I'm afraid not. Frank Jessop is dead, as you say, and I may be at least partly responsible. I should never have said what I did to Dr. Allen, but I hoped that Frank would confide in him himself.'

'Yes, I know that, Vicar, but I can't see where your responsibility lies. Jessop was killed by a bull that went mad. You had nothing to do with that.' Mott considered how it had been. Jessop's body had been found by a motor-cyclist on his way to work the following morning, and, though the bull was grazing peacefully by the roadside, the blood on its horns marked it clearly as the culprit. It had been destroyed, as had one of the cows which had broken a leg, apparently trying to kick its way out of the byre. Something had driven the animals insane with terror that night. 'But perhaps, if Jessop had not been in such a disturbed condition after your question, he might have been able to control the animal, Mr. Mott.'

'Oh, I'm not blaming you or Tom Allen. I am the only person to blame. I wanted help, you see. I wanted people to believe me, and I didn't realize that I can't involve anybody else. I must face this thing alone till I am quite sure what it is.'

'But we want to help, Vicar. Everybody does.' Mott was almost shouting into the mouthpiece. 'Can't you realize that?'

'Yes, I realize it, and I'm very, very grateful. All the same, I have nothing else to say for the time being.' There was a sudden click and the line went dead.

So that was that. Mott replaced the instrument and returned to the dining-room, frowning slightly at Tom Allen. During the last few days the village had been choked with reporters and the Crown was becoming an impossible place to work in. Mary had naturally offered to put him up, but he had the odd feeling that Tom resented his presence. Very strange. One would have thought he would have liked a bit of civilized company. It must be imagination, and the fellow was merely shy and ill at ease. He pushed the thought out of his mind, and sat down at the breakfast table.

'He wouldn't tell you anything?'

'Not a thing, my dear. He says that he is protecting Jessop's memory, but there's more to it than that. He rambled on about having to be sure about something or other, before he can involve anyone else.' Mott knocked back the rest of his coffee. 'The usual stuff in the paper, I suppose?'

'Yes, the same drivel as yesterday, only a lot more of it. I really think everybody is going out of their mind. Oh, yes, there've been some strange things happening: the *Dalecrest*, Joe Bates, and the bull killing Jessop, but I'm perfectly sure that every one of them will be found to have a quite separate and rational explanation. This rubbish is going to lead to mass hysteria, if it's allowed to continue.'

Tom scowled with disgust at the front page of the *North Eastern Gazette*. Since the discovery of the *Tinker-Taylor* and her terrible cargo, the newspapers had really let themselves go. 'THE DUNSTON-HOLME TERROR . . . ARE FLYING SAUCERS RESPONSIBLE? . . . BLACK MASSES ON THE MOORS' had been some of the recent headlines and the present issue appeared to have printed every theory that was offered.

Following the discovery of a survivor's body from the salvage ship, *Dalecrest*, Inspector Basil Jones of the County Constabulary made this statement: 'It is obvious that Daniels was picked up by the catamaran from some floating wreckage. Nobody can say exactly what happened after that, but it seems to me that he must have been mentally deranged by his terrible experience. Yes, it is probable that he killed Rails and Dander, and then made an end of himself in a fit of remorse, but at this stage of the investigation, I can make no further comment.'

'Thank you. I will have a spot more coffee, please. It's quite delicious.' Mott pushed his cup across to Mary. 'But what's wrong with that? It sounds reasonable enough to me.'

'That bit may be, but listen to this.' Tom turned to the next page which contained the picture of an aged crone glowering from a cottage doorway.

Miss Martha Shipton, a direct descendant of Mother Shipton, the famous sixteenth-century prophetess and white witch, gave our reporter this exclusive interview.

'There is a great and terrible power hanging over this place. I have said so for years, but nobody would listen to me. Now it is coming into the light: the hand of the Lord who is never mocked. Colonel Keith was a blasphemer, and God's finger made Joseph Bates let go of that chair. The crew of the *Dalecrest* were libertines who profaned our village, and they were driven mad. Frank Jessop was a drunkard, so it was ordained that a beast should destroy him.'

The editor assures his readers that Miss Shipton's views are not held by the *North Eastern Gazette*. Miss Shipton also stated that a Black Magic cult existed in Dunstonholme and revolting ceremonies had taken place on the moors.

'Cor, stone the crows! Old Martha Shipton has been in and out of loony-bins for years. Do you want to hear any more?'

'Yes, I think I do, Tom.' Mott had been ramming tobacco into a short blackened pipe, which he now lit with considerable ceremony. 'Please read on.'

Alderman Tubman, an active member of the Rural District Council and senior partner of Tubman & Clarke, wine and spirit merchants, stated as follows: 'To me at least, it appears certain that extra-terrestrial forces are at work around Dunstonholme. During my evening rambles over our lonely hills, I have often observed strange lights in the sky and had the uncanny feeling that I was being studied by hostile intelligences which are not of this world.'

'God Almighty! How can they print such stuff? I know all about Tubman's evening rambles, and he doesn't take them alone. There are two paternity orders against him already.' Tom looked with disgust at Mott's pipe which was filling the room with choking grey smoke. He had stopped smoking until after lunch himself, and resented it bitterly. He turned to the next column and disgust became nausea.

Mr. J. Moldon Mott, the world-famous explorer and man of letters, who is staying in the village, was kind enough to give his views. 'There is a strong possibility that the loss of the *Dalecrest* and the deaths of Colonel Keith and Mr. Jessop may somehow be connected, as are other events that happened in the distant past. I have no intention of saying what I consider the connection to be till I have more evidence. But if it exists . . .' [Mr. Mott paused for a moment at this point and raised his hand in emphasis – a hand which had grasped the summits of the world's highest mountains, and hacked its way through impenetrable jungles.] 'If it exists, you may rely on me to discover what it is.'

'You gave them permission to write that?'

'Naturally I did, Doc. It happens to be true.' Mott leaned far back in the frail Chippendale chair, until Tom feared he would crack it.

'I do intend to get to the bottom of this business, and I have already started work. I am now almost certain that there is a connection; a chain of events, if you like, which have one secondary cause.' He pulled a notebook out of his pocket.

'Now, let's consider them one by one. A religious sect named the Children of Paul who arrived here in the first year of the fourteenth century, and massacred the villagers and the castle garrison when they were refused transport to the Feyne Islands. A railway line which was abandoned in 1847. A recluse who was trampled to death by a flock of sheep at about the same time. A lead mine started in 1880, and abandoned the same year. Don't you see how there might be a connection between them and the recent events that have taken place?'

'No, I'm afraid I don't.' Tom looked at his watch. 'In any case I've got my surgery in a few minutes, so I'd better get along.' Mary had been staring at Mott with rapt attention, thereby increasing her husband's annoyance.

'In a moment, Tom, but bear with me a little longer. It won't do your patients any harm to wait.' Mott got up and paced across the room.

'We can't say much about the massacre, as it happened so long ago, but it does appear likely that the villagers took refuge in the castle when these people arrived, and the walls were breached by a mine. In any event, it was never used as a place of defence again.

'There is a good deal of factual evidence about two of the other happenings, though. I spent a busy day in Tynecastle library yesterday, and this is what Thompson's *History of the Border Lines* has to say about the railway:

'The project was a subsidiary of George Hudson's "Empire", which subscribed a capital of £450,000, and was to have run from the main line at Welcott to a terminus at Dunstonholme which was the centre of a prosperous fishing industry at the time.

Work was started in March 1844 and proceeded steadily from Welcott, till Mossgill Moor was reached almost exactly a year later. From then on, the company was faced with constant troubles: frequent accidents taking place, and the men refusing to work in the cutting which they claimed was unsafe. The engineer in charge, Sir Herbert Sunderland, dismissed these claims as being completely unfounded, but labour conditions deteriorated rapidly. At one point riots in the camp necessitated the military being called in. Though higher rates of pay were offered, and workmen recruited from other parts of the country, the unrest continued till January 1847, when work was abandoned and the company went into liquidation.'

Mott flicked on through his notes.

'Now, let's take the lead mine. The official reason for its closure was that the rock was loose and dangerous, but there's an old man in the village named Sims, whose grandfather worked there. Sims remembers his mother telling him how he came home one evening, long before knock-off time. She remonstrated with him over this, and though normally a good-natured man, he swore at her. "Damn you, woman," he said. "You've no idea what it's like in that shaft. There's an evil about the place that can fell a man: a cold in the rock that shrinks your soul as well as your body."'

'You know, I think I'm beginning to understand.' Mary nodded. 'Pounder, the recluse, was quarrying the rock too. Would he have used explosives?'

'I don't know, but he might have had gunpowder.' Mott stopped his pacing and he stared across at Tom. 'Don't you see the connection at last? A castle that was mined, a railway cutting being driven through the moors, a shaft dug for lead. And recently there has been a salvage operation in which the hull of a wreck was blown open. Isn't there one thing that links them to each other?'

'We can't be sure yet.' The pieces were fitting together in Tom's head, but he wasn't going to commit himself yet. 'You mean the use of explosives?'

'That's part of it, but only part. The Children of Paul may have had gunpowder to break into the castle, though it's pretty unlikely, to say the least. The first recorded use of cannon in British history was during Edward III's campaign against the Scots, twenty-seven years later. What I'm getting at is this.' Mott pushed away his notes and stared out of the window. The promise of another fine day was fading fast, and clouds had drifted in across the bay.

'From the little information we have to hand, it appears that these manifestations of terror, or madness, or what you will, only take place after the earth has been disturbed.'

It was over half an hour since he had replaced the telephone, but David Ainger still stood beside it, looking at the mementoes of his life: the books, the crucifix, photographs of dead climbers, and the silver cup which had been presented to him by the Italian Alpine Club for his part in the ascent of Monte Varna. They had given him a great deal of pleasure in the past, but today they appeared quite unimportant.

Time was getting on. Behind him, the old grandfather clock struck nine and Ainger glanced at the calendar on his desk. In a few days he would know for certain if he were insane or not, but he couldn't wait that long. The events of the last week made further waiting unthinkable.

As though coming to a sudden decision, he walked quickly across the room and pulled open a cupboard by the window. The familiar smells of dubbin, leather and manilla hemp gave him a strange feeling of comfort and well-being, and he smiled at the ice axe, the rows of boots, and the hundred and twenty foot rope. A good rope that had been, and though old and worn like himself now, it was still serviceable enough. The last time he had used it and the axe together had been on Ben Nevis in '44: the Tower Ridge with a blizzard blowing, and he and Timmy Slater leading alternate pitches. Not a bad effort for two fifty-year-old men. He took out the rope and the axe and laid them on the table. Timmy was dead of course. He had fallen from the Girdle Traverse on Tryfan, which was a crazy limb to have attempted solo at his age. All his real friends were dead, and how he wished there was just one of them left to help him. How he wished there was one person he could really trust and rely on.

But so there was. There was always one friend when you

wanted him. Ainger smiled at his own forgetfulness and bowed his head before the crucifix.

'Help me, Lord,' he said. 'Help me to find the truth today. Show me if I am merely insane, or if the Devil does exist in this place.' He returned to the cupboard, pulled out a pair of boots, and began to prepare himself for his last climb.

CHAPTER EIGHT

By four o'clock that afternoon, Tom realized that he had had one hell of a day. The morning surgery was the busiest he could remember for the time of the year, with a queue stretching out into the street, though there had been few genuine physical complaints among his patients. Plenty of mental disturbances, however, and plenty of demands for pep pills, sleeping pills, tranquillizers and paternal reassurance.

'Not a wink I've had, Doctor Allen, since that ship blew up. You must give me something.'

'I just can't seem to concentrate any more after reading those stories in the paper. Are those Purple Hearts they talk about any good?' As he wrote the prescriptions, Tom wished he owned a part share in the chemist's shop.

'Do you think it's true what old Martha Shipton says, Doctor, and there really is a curse on the place? Our poor Jenny here gets sick in her stomach just from thinking about it.' The normally level-headed citizens of Dunstonholme appeared to be turning into a race of compulsive neurotics.

Yes, one hell of a day. He had been an hour late for his lunch, and not even allowed to finish it, because the daughter of one of his paying patients had telephoned demanding his immediate attendance. Her father, a retired ship-owner named Harbin, had had a stroke and was at death's door. Tom had driven five miles down the coast to see him and found that her words were true in a manner of speaking. Something had struck Harbin all right: the contents of an empty whisky bottle that lay wedged between the sofa cushions on which he lay groaning, which was strange because the man had always claimed to be a staunch teetotaller. After Tom had given him an emetic and supervised the revolting details of recovery, Harbin had raved about blue demons coming out of the sea to destroy him.

But he might get a little peace now. He looked at his watch as he parked the car in the drive. Still a couple of hours to the evening surgery, and though it was a dull, cloudy day, it would be pleasant to do a bit of gardening. He opened the door and his hopes were rudely shattered by a large black and white animal which leapt up at his shoulders and almost threw him backwards down the steps. 'And who on earth are you?' The dog was enormous already, but judging by the size of its paws, it still had a lot of growing to do. It appeared to imagine that he liked its unwelcome attentions and a long pink tongue ran across his face.

'That is Belford Bugler, soon to be the pride of the Redesdale Foxhounds. Down, boy.' Mott snapped his fingers and the animal left Tom and stationed itself at his feet, gazing up at him with adoration.

'Though still a puppy, and boarded out with Mr. Wilson at the post office, Bugler is said to come from good stock and I am hoping he will be able to assist me in my search for the vicar. A bloodhound would have been more traditional, of course, but it's a question of beggars not being choosers.'

'The vicar? What's happened to him?' Tom goggled at Mott's appearance which was a mixture of the comic and the sinister. He wore a sky-blue anorak, a pair of tight leather shorts which would have got him a stiff fine for indecency from a Spanish magistrate, and scarlet stockings protruded from the tops of his rubber-soled climbing boots. A rope and a haversack were draped over his shoulders, and the pouched belt at his waist contained a hammer and a row of steel spikes.

'That we don't know, but it appears he has disappeared; left the vicarage soon after breakfast and took his climbing gear with him. Mrs. Diver, his daily help, and Mary have gone to fetch me a piece of his clothing which may be of assistance to Bugler – there they are now.'

'Oh, darling, I'm so glad you're back.' Mary hurried into the house, followed by a small, red-faced woman who had obviously been weeping. 'We've been so worried.'

'But why shouldn't Mr. Ainger go out for a bit, if he felt like it? He's probably just gone for a walk.'

'But he didn't tell me where he was going, Doctor. He always does that. He didn't even say that he'd be out for lunch.' Mrs. Diver handed Mott a leather glove. 'I do hope this will help you, sir.

'Yes, he always says when he'll be out, Dr. Allen. Twelve years I've worked for Father Ainger, and I can't remember him not telling me once. I thought he was still in the study, till I brought him his coffee at eleven. Then, I saw that the cupboard was open and he'd taken the axe and that old rope with him.' She blew her nose and wiped away a tear.

'And he promised he'd never go climbing again, after he had that fall in Scotland nine years ago. That shook him up badly, and he's an old man and not strong, as you know, Doctor. Seventy-two he'll be next birthday. Jane Metcalfe told me that her little boy saw him walking up that path to the moors at about half past nine. Oh, I'm that worried, Mrs. Allen. I can just picture him lying hurt under some horrible crag at this very moment.'

'But you must stop worrying, Mrs. Diver.' Mary put an arm around her shoulder. 'Mr. Mott and my husband are going to look for Father Ainger, and I'm sure he will be quite all right.

'You will, won't you, Tom? I telephoned Doctor Medway and he'll do your surgery.'

'I suppose I'd better.' Tom nodded. Ainger was an old fool, and he could easily have hurt himself. Though his heart and chest were sound enough, there was a slight Parkinson's condition which made even hill walking a risk.

'I'll just go and get a few things together.' He hurried into his office and collected a first-aid kit and a light folding stretcher.

'That the lot?' Mott had lowered his haversack and he took the package from Tom, looking admiringly at the stretcher. 'Nice little gadget. It should just go in with a bit of luck. Yes.' He closed the flap and slung the haversack back on to his shoulders. 'Well, shall we go?'

'Yes, but don't you think we should get Ken Rutter to come along with us?'

'Rutter?' Mott frowned as he slipped a lead through Bugler's collar. 'Oh, you mean the local bobby. No, he'd just hold us back, great fat fellow.

'And you are not coming either, my dear.' He shook his head and smiled at Mary. 'The Doc and I will make much better time on our own. Now don't you worry, Mrs. Diver, we'll have the vicar back safe and sound before you know it.

'Come on then, boy. Hy-seek, hy-seek.' He held the glove out to the hound as Tom kissed Mary, and marched purposefully out of the house.

Bugler found the scent almost at once, and after giving two short excited barks, he got down to business and headed inland. As they crossed the square, children stared curiously at Mott's costume, but they were soon out of the village and on to the main road. The hound paused for a moment there, the smells of oil and rubber apparently confusing him, and then turned towards a stile on the other side. There was a path beyond the stile, leading straight up the hillside, but it petered out after a few hundred yards into a wilderness of bracken and young heather. Tom's shoes slipped and twisted on the slope, but Mott's huge boots pounded remorselessly on like pistons and Bugler strained at the leash, now and then giving a little whimper of excitement.

'We're on the right track, it seems.' Mott stopped suddenly and looked down. Though the ground was hard and dry, there was the clear imprint of a climbing boot by his feet.

'Yes, quite a good pull for an elderly man, and I'd give a lot to know what he's up to.' Mott took a map from the pocket of his anorak.

'According to this, the whole district is dotted with small crags, and if he was merely intending to do a bit of scrambling, there are a dozen places he could have been heading for. I doubt the scrambling idea, though. In fact, I'd bet you a year's royalties that the old boy had something much more serious in mind. Not many people come up here, judging by the lack of paths.'

'Very few, I imagine.' Tom was feeling better for the breather.

'One or two shepherds, of course, though a lot of the moor is fenced off from animals. It's supposed to be full of bogs.'

'I can well believe that. Looks like an almost perfect watershed, though they can't be very dangerous after all the dry weather we've been having recently

'Come on, boy. We're still relying on you.' Mott shook Bugler's lead and the hound hurried on with another yelp of excitement.

They were soon at the top of the hill. A crumbling stone wall ran along its crest, and beyond it the moor stretched endlessly away before them. To the west they could see the main road and the railway line, but to the north there was nothing but the moor; empty and deserted, except for a few grazing sheep, curlews wheeling over the heather, and now and then grouse bucketing past them like cannon-balls, with cries of 'Go-back, go-back, go-back'. The cloud was much lower now and drifting trails of mist hung over the scattered outcrops of rock on the horizon, making them look like castles left smouldering after a raid.

Yes, a grim countryside, Tom thought, as he trudged on. He had lived in Dunstonholme for three years, but he still didn't feel a part of it. A country of ballad, and legend, and small bloody wars that had added nothing to history. Border raids, and the Moss Troopers, and two ravens perched on a wall waiting to pluck out the dying knight's eyes. The Children of Paul with a mad monk at their head pouring down into the valley like wolves. He had a sudden feeling of unreality, as though they were crossing some lost, fairy-tale land that had never supported human life. Even the heather had an unnatural grey tinge.

They had been walking for just over an hour when they reached the fence, but it wasn't much of a barrier. The wire had rusted through in places and lay on the ground, though warning notices were nailed to the rotting posts. Just beyond it was the first bog; a patch of green slime, fifty yards wide, which was surrounded by dispirited-looking ferns, and gave off a sweet cloying smell. They were half way round it, when Bugler suddenly whined and sat down.

'Come on, boy. Hy-seek.' Mott held out the glove, but the animal appeared to have given up all interest in the chase.

'Damn, he's lost the scent. Only to be expected with this stench around.' Mott consulted his map again. 'Still, I don't think there's any need to worry. My guess is that Ainger could only have been making for that place with the comic name, Pounder's Hole, which is just over there.' He jerked the dog to its feet and headed towards two parallel rows of crags on the horizon.

'Um, Friend Pounder must have certainly appreciated his privacy, if he wanted to live up here.' The cliffs before them were less than seventy foot high, but their worn, rounded crests made them look like the gaping jaws of some prehistoric monster. 'Give you the creeps, don't they?'

'They certainly do.' Tom turned up his collar against the swirling mist. 'And, much against my better judgement, I'm beginning to admit the possibility of the sheep story.' The crags formed a narrow valley, and beyond it was a wide, grass-covered space ending in a scree shoot. If somebody had been standing in the narrow part of the valley and a flock of sheep grazing at the far end had stampeded, he could easily have been trampled to death.

'Yes, it's possible enough. Granted that something really terrified the poor brutes out of their wits. Ah, good for you, Belford Bugler.' Mott grinned as the hound suddenly gave tongue and strained at the leash. 'Got the scent again, have you?' He broke into a trot after him, the thick bracken tearing at his legs, and now and again more grouse rocketing out of the heather with shrill warnings of 'Go-back, go-back, go-back . . .' As they got nearer, Tom could see that the cliffs were limestone, but so dark with moisture that they looked like black basalt in the mist.

'All right. Go on by yourself, boy, if that's what you want.' Mott slipped the leash, and the hound bounded towards a boulder by the left wall of the valley, where he halted and gave a long, mournful bay.

'Yes, my hunch was right, then.' Mott bent down and picked up a worn and faded rucksack with the initials D. A. stitched on the flap. 'The old fool did come here, and that, I imagine, is the "Hole". Let's hope he hasn't broken his neck in it. I'll give a lot to know what he's up to.' Mott moved towards the cave. It was quite wide and almost half as high as the cliff, but very short, being blocked by a pile of boulders which had fallen from the roof hundreds of years ago. In front of the boulders a shaft led straight down into the earth.

'Mr. Ainger. Are you there, Mr. Ainger?' There was no answer, but at the lip of the shaft Mott saw a line of recent scratches that had obviously been made by climbing boots.

'Yes, he's down there, and I suppose I'll have to go after him, though I've never enjoyed caving.' Mott took off his haversack and uncoiled the rope.

'Can you tie a bowline? Good. Then fix yourself to that rock, and hold me over your shoulder.' He took out a miner's helmet fitted with a lamp, and tucked the first-aid pack into his anorak.

'No, I'm sorry, Tom.' He smiled and shook his head. 'I quite appreciate that you'd like to come too, but I want you to stay up here and hold me in case of mishaps. This rope is a hundred and fifty foot long, but we've no idea how deep the shaft is. Some of these limestone formations are enormous. Just hold me nice and tight and pull like hell if I shout. If the rope runs out we may have to try another way.' Mott tied himself on and sat down on the edge of the shaft.

'When I want to come back, I'll give three sharp tugs. Here goes, then.' He swung his feet on to the opposite wall and started to lower himself down.

At first it was easy. The shaft was smooth and almost vertical, but the walls were just the right distance apart, and he negotiated it in the classic manner: back and hands pressed against one wall, boots on the other; lower right foot – lower buttocks; lower left foot – lower buttocks. It was far safer than crossing a road, and in a few minutes he was standing in a chamber fifty feet below the surface.

Yes, all the area must be practically hollow. As his lamp swept around the cavern he could see at least three exits in the walls, and from one of them there came the sound of running water. No wonder the moor had been fenced off. There would be shafts and crevasses everywhere.

Damn Ainger though! He would have taken that one. The cave twisted slightly to the left and a line of scratches led to a narrow

crack in the floor. He must be a hell of a tough old boy to have
gone down there, and at first glance Mott saw that he would have
to negotiate it head first. He didn't like that, and as he had admitted
to Tom, he didn't like caving either. As a precocious six-year-old
he had borrowed Conan Doyle's *Tales of Terror* from an uncle's
library, and 'Blue John Gap' had given him many a bad dream.

A curious rock formation this. Limestone with what looked like
volcanic ash set in ribs on the walls and, here and there, a glitter of
some metal ore. Vegetation too; though there was precious little
light coming down the shaft, lichen and ferns were growing.

But what was he thinking of? Somewhere below him an old man
might be lying badly injured, and he was considering geology and
botany. He checked that the first-aid kit was secure and lowered
himself towards the crack.

God, it was a tight squeeze! There was scarcely room for his
shoulders, and the rock was rough and clutched at the anorak. At
any moment he felt he would be wedged like a cork in the neck of
a bottle. He braced his legs and wriggled on.

Yes, a bit better now, and the angle was becoming easier. About
sixty degrees and the ceiling was just high enough for him to crawl
down it on his knees. The air appeared to be all right, too, though
there was a strong stench of rotting vegetation. He tried to work
out how far he had come. Fifty feet down the shaft, twenty across
the cave, say another forty after that. He'd be running out of rope
soon, and he wished that he'd brought another light line which
could be fixed to a piton.

What was that? His fingers clutched something soft and clammy
and what looked like a human face leered out at him in the glare
of his lamp. Only a patch of fungus, of course, but he distinctly
heard a voice in his head say – 'What is it? The monster that lives
in Blue John Gap?'

Ah, much better. The tunnel suddenly heightened, so that he
could stand upright, and there was another line of scratches to
show that Ainger had been there. It was wide enough for him to
release the rope; there could only be a few feet left, and the floor
was almost level. He hurried on and stepped out into a second
cavern.

The place was huge, as big as a fair-sized church with stalactites hanging from the ceiling, and a forest of stalagmites standing in a miniature lake of clear water that looked slightly pink in the lamplight. If Pounder's Hole was ever exploited as a tourist attraction, it could provide somebody with a very comfortable living. There had obviously been a big opening in the far wall, but it was blocked by a pile of loose rock. Among the rocks, something metallic glinted.

Yes, Ainger was about all right. The ice axe was wedged against two rocks and it looked as though he had been trying to tunnel a way through. Almost succeeded too. There was a slight gap in the right-hand corner of the pile, and beyond it, Mott fancied he could see the beginning of another shaft leading down.

But where was the man himself? Mott's helmet swept around the cave. 'Mr. Ainger, are you . . .' He started to call out, and then broke off abruptly. He didn't know why, but it was as though he had suddenly been gagged – as though some sixth sense was warning him to keep quiet. He also had a strange feeling of relief that the soles of his boots were rubber.

But there – over there. There was a line of scratches on the floor and he followed them till he was standing beside the little lake. The water really was pink, and all at once he knew that it was no trick of the torchlight that made it appear so. Almost directly below him was a shape which he had first thought to be a rock, but it was moving slightly and dark red streaks were drifting out from it. Ainger had staggered backwards over the edge of the lake and a row of stalagmites had impaled him.

CHAPTER NINE

'I'm sorry, gentlemen, but that's all I can tell you at the moment.' Tom drew back before the reporters. Dunstonholme Cottage Hospital was a tiny institution, with only eight beds, that had been founded by a local philanthropist before the First World War. Its entrance hall was filled to overflowing,

'Mr. Ainger had a fall while pot-holing, and though I presume he died of his injuries, nobody can say more till a proper autopsy has been performed.

'Yes, I agree that it was a foolish thing for him to have done at his age, but rock climbing has always been his hobby. Many of us maltreat our bodies, don't we?' He grinned at the cigarette in his hand.

'No, sir. I am a physician, not a detective, and I can see no connection between the vicar's death and any other events which have taken place recently. And now, if you will excuse me please.' He gave a little bow and drew back into the office, shutting the door behind him.

'But what did he die of, Tom?' The door had been open, and Mary had heard everything that was said. 'You told me that the actual injuries from his fall couldn't have killed him.'

'I don't know, darling.' Tom stubbed out his cigarette. He hadn't felt so tired since the days when, as a young ship's surgeon, he had been put ashore at Cochin to help fight a cholera epidemic.

'All I'm certain of is that Ainger didn't die from his fall. Those injuries from the stalagmites look pretty impressive, but not one of them could have been fatal, and from what Mott told me his face was above water, so he couldn't have been drowned either. My guess is that he was dead before he even reached the lake.'

'Heart failure from the exertion then? But you always told me that Ainger's heart was quite remarkable for his age – as good as a man's in the prime of life.'

'That's true enough, and the autopsy will show it. He was in excellent physical condition for his age, apart from that Parkinson's condition which usually tends to prolong life. His heart just stopped for no apparent reason and he fell back into the lake; dead before he even hit the stalagmites.'

'But that's ridiculous. There's always a reason.'

'Yes, there is always a reason, but sometimes it is not apparent. We often get quite inexplicable deaths from sudden vagal inhibitions, for instance.

'You should remember the famous case of the Scottish students. During a rag, they built a dummy guillotine and went through all the motions of execution with an unfortunate janitor. When he was tied to the block and a wet towel suddenly flicked across his neck, he died instantly.'

'You mean Ainger died of shock?'

'I think he was killed by extreme terror, my dear.'

Tom looked through the glass partition. The journalists were filing away down the steps and the hall was empty.

'I could hardly tell them that, though. This village is becoming a mad house, as it is. Parents keeping their children away from school – queues outside the surgery demanding tranquillizers – tales of flying saucers and little green men from Mars – that old trouble maker, Martha Shipton, talking about the hand of God. It just needs one more story to start complete mass hysteria.'

'Yes, you are quite right of course.' Mary suddenly reached out and took his hand. 'It must have been terrible for you up there.'

'It was terrible for Mott, not me. He went down and brought Ainger up.' Though he still resented Mott's presence in his house, Tom was beginning to respect him deeply.

'Yes, that must have taken a lot of guts.' He remembered his feelings as he had waited at the top of the shaft. The rope being slowly paid out and suddenly going slack, the hound snuggling against his side, and the mist thickening into a blanket across the mouth of the cave. He had experienced anxiety, and then dread, and always intense curiosity. Why on earth had Ainger gone down there? What did he hope to find? Then at last had come three tugs on the rope and a few minutes later Mott had climbed to the surface. It had needed all their joint strength to pull Ainger's body up the shaft, and his face had reminded him of a biblical quotation, as it appeared over the edge: 'a leper, as white as snow'.

'He died of fear.' Mary looked out of the window. Though it was after midnight, almost every building in the village was still lit up.

'Darling, you said that this place is becoming a mad house, and I think I'm one of the maniacs. It may be all nonsense about Martians and the hand of God, but something horrible is happening here. There must be a connection between all these deaths. The crew of the *Dalecrest*, Keith, Frank Jessop, and now Ainger. There must be a common reason for them.'

'And why should Ainger have gone up there anyway? He hadn't done any climbing for years, so why did he go today and not tell anybody? What was he hoping to find?'

'Nobody knows that, but Mott has gone to the vicarage. There might be a diary, or some papers to give us a clue.' Tom glanced at his watch. 'But I'm damned tired. Let's say good night to Matron, and then go home.'

'Very well, but I'd like to see him first.' Mary picked up her handbag. 'I was very fond of the old chap, and I'd like to have one last look, before they take him to Welcott in the morning.'

'All right, though he's not a pleasant sight.' Tom led the way down the corridor, and opened the door of the tiny mortuary. Ainger's body appeared to have shrunk in death, and it hardly raised a bulge under the sheet.

'Oh, my God.' Mary swayed against the trolley as Tom pulled back the sheet, and for a moment, he thought she was about to faint.

'The eyes! And his colour too! His face is so white, darling. He looks as though he'd seen the Gorgons and been turned to stone.'

'Stop it.' Tom pulled her away. 'Don't look at him, if it upsets you so much. There is quite enough hysterical behaviour in this village without our adding to it. Ainger died of shock, and there is probably a perfectly normal explanation. The rock might have moved when he was trying to cut a way through it, and made him think he was being buried alive. He could have had a sudden attack of claustrophobia. Anything might have happened.' He started to replace the sheet, but Mary gripped his arm.

'Yes, Tom. He died of shock, but I think that there is something you've missed.' Her voice was quite controlled again as she stared down at the body. 'Look at his right hand.'

'What about it?' Tom leaned forward. 'Oh, you mean the scratch. It's not important. He might have got it when he fell, or when he was climbing down.' He suddenly felt his body stiffen, as he saw what she was looking at. Ainger's hand was tightly clenched, but just visible between the thumb and the index finger was the end of a knot of reddish hair.

'The key to the laboratory, Dr. Allen? At this hour of the night?' Miss Nesbett raised her very considerable eyebrows. She had held her position for over twenty years and was a firm believer in the principle that doctors might come and go, but she went on for ever. 'It's well after midnight.'

'I realize that, Matron, but it is extremely important that I make some tests.' Tom pronounced the title with a flourish. The old battle-axe had about as much right to it as a tug-boat skipper to 'captain', but he knew how much she valued her dignity.

'I see.' She lifted a key from a hook above her desk, but didn't hand it to him. 'And while we're alone, Doctor, I'd like to ask you why the vicar's body was brought here, and not taken directly to Welcott where the post mortem will naturally be conducted. Surely that would have been the correct procedure?'

'It would have been the usual procedure, Matron, but I wanted to examine the body myself first. Now, may I have the key please?'

'In a moment, Dr. Allen, but I hope you realize that I am duty bound to make a full report to the governing body. This hospital is a voluntary institution dedicated to the sick of the district. It was never intended to be used as a mortuary.'

'I'm aware of that, but I shall take full responsibility for everything. The key, Matron.'

'Very well, Doctor, but I do hope you won't be long. I am quite on my own tonight and extremely busy.' There were only three patients in the building, all of them fast asleep. She knew that Tom must be aware of this, but the pretence of activity had to be maintained.

'Here is the key, but please let me know when you have finished. I like to make sure that everything is properly locked up.'

'I'll do that, Matron.' Tom almost snatched it out of her hand and hurried down the corridor to where Mary was waiting for him.

Like 'Matron', the title 'Laboratory' was a courtesy; it consisted of a small room with a sink and a couple of benches, and most of the equipment was out of date. There was quite a modern microscope though, and Tom switched on a lamp beside it.

'Now, let's see if we can place this.' He slid the knot of hair into position and turned the fine adjustment. As the picture came into

focus, the individual hairs looked like the trunks of trees, brought
down by a hurricane and piled on top of each other.

'No, they're not human. I don't think so anyway.' The hairs
were as thick and bristly as quills, though the papilla and follicles
resembled those of a man. What was the thing that Ainger had
encountered in the cavern? Unpleasant images of prehistoric
monsters and sub-men flitted through Tom's head, as he studied
them. Then he pulled the lamp a little closer and grinned, seeing
the characteristic reddish tinge shine out at him.

'There's your monster, darling; just a fox. Have a look for yourself. There must be another easier entrance to the cave and some
old vixen had her earth down there. She rubbed off a bit of fur on
the rocks and Ainger picked it up.'

'Yes, I see. It does look like a fox.' Mary frowned as she bent
over the microscope. 'But the hairs seem diseased somehow. They
appear to be almost succulent at the bottom.'

'Let me look.' Tom took her place. 'Yes, I think I know what it is.
It's a condition caused by over-activity of the sweat glands. I can't
remember what it's called, but the disease was endemic in Poland
during the last century.' He broke off and stood staring at her with
an expression of complete bewilderment on his face.

'No, not a fox then. Foxes don't sweat through the skin.'

CHAPTER TEN

'A terrible lot of books Father had, Mr. Mott. Took a tidy bit of
dusting, I can tell you. I did my best to keep them decent, but he
was always trying to stop me coming in here; said I mixed things
up.' Mrs. Diver laid another cup of coffee on the table. 'Do you
think he could have read them all, sir?'

'I'm quite sure he did.' Mott looked admiringly at the titles.
A damned fine library for a country parson, he thought. Not
merely theology. From the little he knew of Ainger, he would
have expected that. Just as he would have expected the occult and
medical sections that Tom had mentioned. But in this case was
an extensive selection of general scientific works ranging from

botany – there was Large's *Advance of the Fungi* – to telepathy and extrasensory perception. Yes, Rhine and Upton Sinclair were on the top shelf, and next to them was Komroff's *Electromagnetism in Living Tissue*. He pulled it out and glanced at the marginal notes. Old Ainger had really gone to town on that one.

'But isn't it time you went to bed, Mrs. Diver?' He replaced the book and smiled at her. 'You've had a very trying day and it's well after midnight.'

'I know that, sir, but I'd rather stay here, if you don't mind.' She stifled a sob with her handkerchief. 'I've had a room with my sister since my husband died, but I couldn't sleep tonight. Besides, I'd like to clear up after you've finished, Mr. Mott.'

'That's very kind of you, but it will be quite a job, I'm afraid.' Mott winced slightly. The room looked as though it had been ransacked by a burglar. Cupboards were pulled open, drawers had spilled their contents on the floor, and the desk and table were littered with papers. Ainger had been a great hoarder and there were letters and bills and sermons running back over ten years. Not one of them had helped him at all.

'What exactly is it that you are looking for, sir?'

'I'm not really sure, Mrs. Diver. Something that will tell me why the vicar should have suddenly decided to go up to Pounder's Hole today, perhaps. I think you said that he hadn't done any climbing for years.'

'That's true, Mr. Mott. But do drink your coffee while it's hot, sir.' She pushed the cup a little closer to his hand.

'After Father had that fall in Scotland, he promised me and his sister, Mrs. Royce – she's dead of course – that he'd never climb again. He kept it too; until today.' Once again she pressed the handkerchief to her face. 'What made him do it, Mr. Mott? I know he's been acting very strangely lately, but I never thought he'd go and break a solemn promise.'

'That's what I'm trying to find out, Mrs. Diver.' Mott stirred his coffee thoughtfully. 'When was it that the vicar started to become strange?'

'Well, I wouldn't like to say exactly. It was gradual like, and I don't agree with Doctor Allen putting it all down to this Parkinson's disease, though there's no doubt that those Artene pills did Father a lot of good. There was something worrying him, sir. Sort of preying on his mind, as you might say.

'I suppose it was about four years ago. Just before he bought the typewriter.' She pointed to a battered portable on the desk.

'I see.' Mott stared at the keyboard, as though hoping that it would suddenly start to tap out a message. 'That would have been around the time when the R.A.F. plane crashed up on the moors and they never found the pilot.'

'That's right, sir. Soon after that it was. I was so pleased when he got the typewriter and started on his book. I thought it would take him out of himself and stop him worrying. It didn't though, sir. He seemed to get worse and worse as time went by. Many's the day that I've heard him praying aloud in here, asking God to tell him if he was mad or not.'

'Did you see this book, Mrs. Diver?' Mott's fingers drummed on the edge of the desk. At last he felt that he might be getting somewhere.

'Well, parts of it, sir. He was working at it all the time. Sometimes, when I came in of a morning, he'd be fast asleep by the typewriter with the pages lying all around him.

'I'd hoped that it would be a nice story that people could enjoy, but it was just a dull old history of the village. He used to keep it in that cupboard over there with a lot of pamphlets and things; source material, he called them. It wouldn't interest you, Mr. Mott; just the history of Dunstonholme.'

'On the contrary, Mrs. Diver, it would interest me very much indeed. In that cupboard, you say? I thought I'd been through all of them pretty thoroughly.' Mott was already crossing the room, but she shook her head.

'Oh, it's no good you looking for it, sir. He had two copies, but he sent them both off. There's nothing in the cupboard now.'

'And where did he send them?' Mott turned and frowned down at her. 'Please try and remember, Mrs. Diver. It's extremely important. Who did he send them to?'

'Well, I can't say for sure, sir. One went off some time back, and the other only last week. I was in the room when he made up the parcel. Very strange indeed he was, Mr. Mott. He kept muttering to himself that the only person who could help him was his spiritual superior.'

Dr. Russell Fenge, Lord Bishop of Welcott, sometimes described in the right-wing press as the 'despicable bishop of Welcott', was a liberal churchman and against things. High on the list of his hates were capital punishment, class and race discrimination, nuclear armaments, and the Holy Ghost. He often referred to himself as a rational Christian, and his best-selling work of popular theology, *God Knows*, proved his deep and comforting faith in the impotence of the Deity.

'Ah, Mr. Moldon Mott.' Though it was after eleven o'clock in the morning, he wore a purple dressing-gown which gave him the air of a clerical Noel Coward.

'Come in, my dear fellow.' He held out his ring to be kissed; there were certain rituals of which he approved, and winced slightly as Mott grasped the outstretched hand and shook it.

'Thank you, my lord. It's very decent of you to see me at such short notice.' Mott had heard nothing good about the man, but at least he would grant him that. Besides, he needed his help.

'Not at all. Not at all.' Fenge's smile appeared to be in danger of splitting his jaws. 'As I said at the Pen and Quill dinner only last week, "If thieves can stick together, we literary gents must follow their example." ' Though he hadn't read any of Mott's books, he understood that he was something of a personage. He made a point of cultivating personages, because one never knew when they could be useful.

'Ah, you're admiring my Spätz.' Mott was glowering at a picture over the mantelpiece. 'Nice, isn't it? There is much more strength and maturity there than in his earlier periods.'

'Yes, there's strength all right.' The painting appeared to show a modern workshop in which a number of malformed persons were constructing furniture. One of them was hammering a chair leg into position by brute force. 'What is it supposed to be?'

'It's "Joseph the Craftsman", of course. You can see him in the right background with the halo and the circular saw.'

'Um. He's going to lose a finger soon, if he doesn't put that guard down.' Mott turned away from the picture. 'There's far too much of that simple carpenter business, if you ask me. I follow Sholem Asch's theory that Saint Joseph was a well-to-do timber merchant.'

'Do you indeed?' Dr. Fenge was beginning to feel less warm towards his guest. 'Dear old Asch had many interesting notions. At the same time, as liberally minded men, I feel we must always stress the humble origins of Jesus.'

'How extraordinary.' Mott strongly resented being called a liberal. 'According to my Bible, he was descended from a long line of kings.'

'Ah, but you shouldn't take your Bible too literally, Mr. Mott. As I am pointing out in my forthcoming book, *A Thousand True Crosses*, one must always balance the facts with present-day values.'

'I'm sure you are right, Bishop.' Mott remembered that he wanted Fenge's help, but he was damned if he was going to go on calling him 'my lord'. 'What I came to see you about was a certain typescript that Father Ainger is supposed to have sent you.'

'Ainger – Ainger – Ainger?' Fenge frowned and then suddenly nodded. 'Oh, you mean Ainger from Dunstonholme, of course; poor old Dave. I was so sorry to hear of his death, so very, very sorry.' He looked as sorry as the average person does after hearing about a railway accident in China.

'Yes, poor, poor Dave Ainger. One of God's good men, Mr. Mott. But perhaps a little past his work, to put it charitably. As I told the Home Secretary some time ago, "There is no place for mere goodness in the church of today. The modern parish priest must be as efficient and ruthless as . . ." ' He paused to strengthen the example. ' "As a trade union leader, or the top executive of a nationalized industry." I'm afraid Dunstonholme has run down badly during the last few years. The parish is dominated by a clique of snobbish women who have no thought of increasing the congregation. I shall appoint a good man there. Somebody who will be in tune with the ordinary people and stress that the disciples themselves were also simple fishing folk.'

'I am sure you will, Bishop. But about this manuscript that Mr.

Ainger sent you. It is a work on local history, and, as I am living in the district, I'd very much like to read it. I believe there were two copies.'

'Yes, I think you may be right.' The bishop pressed a bell on his desk. 'Perhaps my chaplain will be able to unearth them. If he can, you are most welcome to a copy, though what a man of your reputation will learn from Dave Ainger's ramblings is beyond me. Ah, there you are, Toby.' A youthful cleric in a frilled cassock had appeared in the doorway. 'Some time ago, you told me that Ainger of Dunstonholme sent us copies of a local history he had compiled. See if you can lay your hands on them, there's a good chap.'

'Certainly, my lord. At once, my lord.' The youth retreated backwards, as though from royalty. 'I'm not quite certain where they are, but I'll do my best not to keep your lordship waiting.'

'You haven't read it yourself, then?' Mott scowled at a signed photograph of Dr. Hastings Banda on the wall.

'Good heavens, no. How could I, Mr. Mott? What with my duties at the House of Lords, foreign missions, the Coloured Neighbours League, and of course my literary efforts, my time is pretty full.' His smile was both boyish and sad. The hero, Alexander, with the cares of the world upon his shoulders.

'No, if I read everything my clerics sent me, life would be quite insupportable. I had a telephone call from the fellow at Redhaven only this morning, complaining about the Mission to Youth scheme. He wanted to expel a couple of high-spirited lads from the club, merely because they put a live rat in the font and it bit his thumb. Doddering old killjoy! Some people would like to bring back public flogging and the stocks.'

'Yes, some people certainly would.' Mott had a sudden pleasant picture of the bishop's fleshy shoulders quivering under the lash. A day in the stocks would do him a power of good too.

'Quite so. The amount of sadism that still exists is very frightening.' Dr. Fenge nodded in agreement. 'But talking shop for a moment, Mr. Mott, the diocese is making a real effort for the Feed the Brains campaign this year, and it strikes me that you're just the kind of chap we're after. As I was saying to the Archbishop only the other day, what we want are men who have knocked about the world and shown the value of liberal leadership. Men that young people respect, but feel quite free to discuss their problems with. "Big Brothers" in fact, though not in poor George Orwell's sinister sense. Well, what about it? I'll make you a group leader if you're interested.'

'No, I'm sorry, Bishop.' Mott fought to control his expression. 'I really am very busy.'

'Ah, pity about that, but perhaps later on . . . And here are your papers, I imagine.' Fenge turned as the door opened again. 'You managed to run them to ground, Toby?'

'Yes, my lord.' The priest minced across the room and laid a dog-eared typescript on the desk. 'This is the second copy, which came last week.'

'Good lad.' Fenge gave his arm a squeeze. 'I really don't know what I'd do without you.'

'Thank you very much, my lord. There was a covering letter which I didn't bother to show you. It was impertinent in the extreme and proved Mr. Ainger to be completely deranged.' Toby had a slight lisp and sniffed at the end of each sentence.

'Did it indeed? Still, de mortuis and all that, Toby, and you should have let me see it, you know. Always remember that I am as accessible to the humblest deacon as I am to the Prime Minister.'

'I'm so sorry, my lord. It's just that your lordship is so overworked that I hate to bother you with trivia.' The chaplain sniffed again and his eyes were watering. Mott wondered if he had a bad cold or was about to burst into tears at the rebuke. 'Shall I read it to you now, my lord?'

'Yes, by all means. But get Mr. Moldon Mott and myself a drink first. Good.' Fenge leaned gracefully back against his desk and inhaled the brandy. 'Now proceed.'

'Thank you, my lord.' Toby picked up a sheet of paper. 'It is undated and he marked it "Private and Confidential".

'My dear Lord Bishop,
    As I have had no acknowledgement of my earlier communication, and have been unable to contact you by telephone, I am afraid that it may

have been lost in the post. I am therefore sending you another copy of my *History of Dunstonholme from the Earliest Times to the Present Day*.

My lord, you are my father in Christ, and I beg you to read this manuscript. I have no literary skill, but please be patient with me and advise me what to do. Tell me if I am insane or whether my conclusions are correct and there really is a terrible danger hanging over our village. I have no one to turn to but you, and time is running out so fast . . .'

Toby broke off with a sudden giggle and glanced at a calendar on the wall.

'Well, go on, my boy. Let Mr. Mott and myself share your merriment.' The bishop raised his eyebrows.

'I'm sorry, my lord.' He fought back another giggle. 'It's just that today's date is the twentieth of June.'

'I am perfectly aware of that, but I can't say that I find anything particularly funny about it.'

'No, of course not. But I think you will do, my lord.' Toby was blushing like a girl. 'Ainger really was as mad as a hatter, it appears. He says that, unless you read his manuscript and act upon it, the world may come to an end on June 24th.'

CHAPTER ELEVEN

No, it was impossible. Such things just didn't happen. Mott had rarely disliked two people as much as he did Bishop Fenge and his chaplain, but he felt he had to agree with them. Ainger must have been right round the bend.

And yet he hadn't written like a madman. Mott scowled across the gloomy reference-room of the Tynecastle public library. He had read the typescript twice now, and he could see that a devil of a lot of work had gone into it. It was an almost complete record of every out-of-the-way occurrence that had taken place in Dunstonholme since the Norman invasion.

Much of the material had been taken from word of mouth of course; legends and folk tales of children and very old people.

George Bridger, an eighty-five-year-old farm labourer, told me that his grandfather was amongst those who had recovered Pounder's body. 'He came into the kitchen, and though an abstemious man, he pulled out a bottle of gin, and he didn't put it back till it was a quarter empty. "It was no accident, whatever people tell you," he said to my mother. "Somebody or something drove those sheep down the valley, and they'd almost trampled the poor devil into the ground."'

A woman, Molly Carlin, had preceded Pounder's intention of living out on the moor during the eighteenth century and had been stoned to death as a witch. Her body was buried just outside the churchyard under a plain slab of granite, and children still believed that, if they ran three times round the square and then knelt down by the slab, they would hear her screaming.

Ainger had got a lot of material from books too, though, and had indexed his references. Mott opened the first volume of Propert's *History of the North-Eastern Railway*. The library had a fine section on local history and the attendants had been very helpful.

Work on the branch line between Welcott and Dunstonholme was finally abandoned in 1847. The generally accepted reasons for the company's failure were constant labour troubles, caused by radical agitators, and lack of capital preceding the collapse of George Hudson's 'Empire'. The author has no wish to contradict these theories completely, but would like to quote a statement made by a foreman ganger named Allan Robson. Robson had worked on railways all over the British Isles and cannot be regarded as a nervous character.

'All went well and smoothly till we started the cutting through Mossgill Moor, and then nothing was ever right again. The Irishmen walked off the job in a body after three days, and I can't say that I blame them. It was just as bad with the local chaps, and I've seen grown men throw down their picks and walk off the job, though their families were well nigh starving. There was something not canny about that place. You had the feeling that you were digging your way through into Hell. Even the soldiers who came to keep order felt it.'

So much for the railway. Mott picked up *The Decline of the Middle Ages* by Benson and Scott which had a chapter on the Children of Paul, with particular reference to their founder, Paul of Ely, or the Young Man from Ely, as he was sometimes called. The authors were violently partisan and anti-Catholic, and claimed on little evidence that Paul was a forerunner of Copernicus who had been persecuted and driven from his monastery on account of scientific curiosity. They stated that the most likely reason for the Dunstonholme massacre was that an evil parish priest had incited the villagers and the castle garrison to attack his followers, and closed with a eulogy. 'It may well be that, below the restless waters of the North Sea, perished a greater genius than Galileo; another victim of superstition and ignorance.'

Yes, insane or not, Ainger had checked his references thoroughly. *Legends of the North-East Coast* gave a detailed account of the local folklore, most of which had an extremely sinister quality; ghosts and demons walking the moors at night, and a monstrous blind thing called the Draken Worm that came out of the sea and carried off children. There was also a short section on the lead mine which bore a marked similarity to the events at the railway cutting.

Yes, Ainger had presented a lot of evidence. But his conclusions! Mott shook his head sadly as he closed the typescript. They were quite absurd. There was no mental or physical force to support them. Ainger had been deranged by too much study and morbid imagination.

And yet – and yet. The word kept running into his thoughts. There certainly did seem to be a connection between the events: some common and extremely evil cause. Mott leaned back in the chair and closed his eyes for a moment.

Could life have maintained itself under such conditions? Could mutations have taken place and nature produced the powers that Ainger claimed must exist? If one granted that, Ainger might very well be right. In four days' time, Hell was quite literally going to be let loose, and he, J. Moldon Mott, would have made a bigger discovery than that of the sources of the Nile.

He opened his eyes and looked up at the library clock. In a short time he had an appointment at the university, but there were still a few minutes to spare. He picked up a volume of the *Newgate Calendar* and turned to the chapter which recounted the long, eventful lives of Mr. and Mrs. Sawney Beane.

'Another double, Landlord, and don't be mean with the bitters this time.' It was two hours later, and Mott leaned heavily against the counter of a saloon bar. He hardly ever visited pubs, except in search of company, but now he felt that he really needed a drink. The room was full of noise, as office workers jostled one another for a quick one before going home, and a steady hum of traffic came through the open door. He was barely conscious of it.

All he could think about was Ainger's typescript, because Ainger could very well have hit on the truth, Mott was almost certain of that now. After leaving the library he had had a long interview with a Mr. Brian Mary Joyce, reader in philosophy at Armstrong College, and author of several standard works on extrasensory perception, and everything was fitting into place.

'My dear, dear man. Of course I believe in communication without the aid of one of the five senses, and I assure you that I'm not a charlatan, a mystic, or a lunatic who thinks that the laws of nature can be broken.' Joyce was a short, bustling Irishman with a goatee beard and an air of extreme prosperity which reminded Mott of the 'poor exile from Erin' who had made good. He had sat very close to Mott on a sofa, and kept poking him in the side to drive home each point he raised.

He had a lot of points, and at the beginning they all seemed dull and inconclusive. He spoke of the work of Rhine and Lewis on telepathy; operators sitting with a screen between them, trying to identify playing cards or numbers, usually with only moderate success; picture reproductions made in different rooms; travellers' tales of Australian aborigines contacting fellow clansmen over hundreds of miles, and African witch-doctors seeing contemporary events over a thousand. Mott felt that he knew much more about these than Joyce, and he had begun to get bored. But at last they came to something which he felt he could accept, in principle at least.

'All matter, Mr. Mott, and that includes the human body, is nothing more than a system of electrical impulses, and the metabolism of the body is largely controlled by emotions. We "go red with anger", for example – he felt fear and "his bowels turned to water", if I may quote from the Good Book. Once you can realize that, everything will start to become as clear as daylight.' Joyce had given Mott another sharp dig in the ribs to emphasize the point.

'Now, Rhine's experiments showed a percentage of success, but not enough to be conclusive, and they proved very little. Recently people have been working on different lines, however. Two or more operators sit behind their screens, but they concentrate on emotions, rather than numbers or objects: anger, love, fear, joy, what you will. And, if the operators are really in tune, the results can be quite astonishing. As many as nine successes out of ten have been recorded.

'Yes, you see the point, don't you?' Again his finger prodded Mott's side. 'In a state of emotion, the electrical impulses in one human body became so strong that they were passed on to another. It has also been found that, if several transmitting agents are employed, the percentage of successes are proportionately higher.

'But that was only the beginning. Two years ago, Boris Komroff in Warsaw realized that proof must be substantiated by failure as well as success, and we must allow the real breakthrough to him.

'What Komroff did was to enclose his transmitting operator in a box screened with lead or some other efficient non-conductor which would absorb the thought waves. It was found that, even with operators who were perfectly in tune, the amount of successes were so small that they could only be explained by simple coincidence.'

'It's possible all right.' Mott muttered the words aloud to the consternation of a barmaid who was serving another customer. A means of contact by electrical impulses that had been stimulated by emotion. And, if the emotion was strong enough – hatred or anger, or perhaps intense fear – there was no knowing how far those impulses might travel.

Yes, Ainger's conclusions could very easily be correct. Mott tried to remember how he himself had felt in the caves. Curiosity at first. They had been much warmer than he had expected, but there was nothing very strange about that. One of the Cheddar caves kept an even temperature summer and winter. The rock formation had been extremely odd, though: limestone and volcanic ash together, and there were lichens and ferns growing from cracks in the walls.

It was in the second shaft that he'd begun to feel fear. The rock had been like a living creature clutching at his body, trying to hold him there for ever, and the fungus had leered at him like a ravaged face. He had had to force himself to go on.

And then there was the big cavern. The pink water in the lake, the rock fall with the ice axe wedged in it, the scratches on the floor, and finally Ainger's body lying on the forest of stalagmites. He had had no time to think then. He had just concentrated on getting Ainger out, but now, as he stood in that crowded bar, he suddenly realized the truth. He knew what must have killed Ainger, what had driven the bull mad, what had destroyed the crew of the salvage ship. He also knew that he had had the luckiest escape of his life.

Yes, it all fitted together. Modern research in extrasensory perception supported Ainger's theory, as did history. And, if the final paragraph of the typescript was correct too, there was very little time left.

Mott glanced at a calendar above the bar. He admired the female form, and normally would have appreciated the picture of an over-developed girl perched on the back of a dolphin, but now he could only think of the date below her. In four days the Gorgons might be going to show their faces.

But how could it be stopped? How the hell could he stop it, short of using poison gas, or blowing up half the district with high explosive? He drained his glass, and pushing aside two tired-looking men who were attempting to get served, strode to the door.

It was a lovely evening and most of the people in the street looked happy, probably thinking of a week-end devoted to beaches, or gardens, or the sun. At the corner a group of musicians had burst into a rousing Dixie-land march, the singer's voice rising stridently above the roar of the traffic.

> Say, Darkies, have you seen the Massa with the moustache on
> his face?
> Go 'long the road some time this morning, like he's got to leave
> the place . . .

Mott grinned sadly at the words and the expressions of the home-going crowds. Unless all the evidence was wrong, unless he could think up something, they wouldn't be looking so happy in four days' time. He stopped smiling as a newspaper van drew up in front of him. The placards on it read ANOTHER DUNSTONHOLME TRAGEDY, and as though in mockery the music rose to a crescendo.

The Massa run – ha-hah, but we shall say hello.
It must be time for kingdom comin', and the Year of Jubilo.

CHAPTER TWELVE

'I don't know. It could have been an accident, I suppose.' Tom pushed aside his cup. He had hardly eaten any supper and he didn't feel like coffee. 'They must have been insane or completely irresponsible to have behaved like that.'

'But, according to what it says here, they were just the opposite.' Mary turned a page of the evening paper. ' "West was a theological student, and Millar, an articled clerk with Chalker & Smith, the Welcott solicitors." They both sound very steady boys indeed.' She pushed the paper across to him and considered what had happened.

The young men were keen members of a motor-cycle club and they had borrowed a friend's van, telling him that they intended to take their unsilenced machines to a place called Salter's Gate to train for a forthcoming scramble. The van had been found parked on the roadside and tyre marks proved that they had ridden their bicycles up on to the moors.

And then they must have changed their plans. The tracks showed that they had turned right at the top of the hill and driven towards the crags by Pounder's Hole. Perhaps morbid curiosity over Ainger's death was the reason, but neither of them could talk about it. Millar was dead and West was lying in hospital, critically ill. All one could say for sure was that, at about midday, the bicycles were seen crossing the moor at high speed. They were abreast and the shepherd who watched them said that he thought the riders must have been drunk. As they approached him, the machines suddenly collided and threw both the boys against a dry stone wall.

'Tom, isn't it like the others? Remember what Mott said about the earth being disturbed. Couldn't the noise of two unsilenced motor-bicycles have the same effect? It looks as though they had both been driven mad. When Mr. Crawford reached West, he tried to fight him off.'

'Yes, he tried to. He had also crawled fifteen yards from the wall which sounds quite incredible.' Tom pulled hard at his cigarette. 'The left lung was punctured, and the skull fractured in three places. When I telephoned Tynecastle Infirmary just now, they told me that they'd had to remove part of his frontal lobe. If the poor devil survives, he'll probably be an imbecile for the rest of his life.

'Oh, darling, what's happening in this place? Why should two perfectly normal boys suddenly behave like maniacs?'

'Because they were maniacs, Tom. It's as simple as that.' They swung around and saw Mott standing in the doorway. 'West and Millar had been driven mad by fear and they were running away. And I think I know what they were running from.' Mott came slowly into the room and he looked tired and much older. There were lines under his eyes and his normally tight, rubbery face was grey and puffy.

'Sorry I dashed off this morning without telling you when I'd be back, but I was in a bit of a hurry. Thank you, my dear. That's exactly what I needed.' He lowered himself into a chair and took a cup of coffee from Mary.

'Yes, I've read about those poor chaps on the motorbikes, and I can tell you this. What happened to them is all part of the same pattern. Like Joe Bates, and the crew of the *Dalecrest*, and the bull that killed Jessop; they were terrified and they were running away. It is now up to us to put an end to the thing that made them run.' He lifted a brief-case and laid it on the table.

'I'll explain myself in a moment, but I'd like to ask you a couple of questions before I start. The first is this: do you believe in the possibility of communication without the direct use of one of the five senses?'

'The possibility?' Tom frowned. 'Yes, I suppose I would admit that, but I'd want a lot of evidence before I even began to regard it as a fact. I did read that Warsaw University have been doing some interesting work on extrasensory perception recently.'

'Yes, they certainly have.' Mott gave them a brief account of what he had learned from Brian Joyce.

'To me, it appears likely that such powers may exist in certain individuals: the communication of emotion to another person by means of electrical impulses from the brain. It also seems reasonable to me that, if more than one transmitting agent is employed, the strength of the impulses will be proportionately greater.' He got up and stared out of the window. Eight o'clock on a lovely June evening, and there were just three more days to Midsummer's Eve: not a single cloud in the sky; with the sunlight lighting up the bay and the soft contours of the hills. The room was very warm, but Mott suddenly shivered and tightened his jacket. It was somehow obscene that all that beauty should screen so much evil.

'Now for my second question. If an individual were suddenly placed in a completely new and hostile environment would you expect changes, both physical and mental, to take place in its make-up?'

'Naturally I would. There are hundreds of instances in the animal and vegetable kingdoms.' What on earth was Mott driving at? Tom wondered. He did look tired, and ill too. The blurbs on his books stated that he was fifty, but he might have been in his late sixties at that moment.

'The classic human examples are wolf-children, of course. The female grey wolf has an abnormally strong maternal urge, and there have been several recorded cases of babies being stolen and adopted by a pack of wolves. The results are not as romantic as the Romulus or Mowgli stories, I'm afraid. There was a very good book on the subject written by a medical missionary in India – I think the title was *The Human Cubs*.' Though he was trying to cut down his smoking, Tom lit another cigarette from the butt of his last one.

'Usually, in such cases, the children die of malnutrition at an early age, or are killed by the young wolves in puppy play. There was one famous instance of survival however. A party of hunters in Northern India shot two adult wolves outside a cave, and went inside to finish off the cubs. When they had done that and were about to leave, they heard a whining noise at the back of the cave, and saw two monstrous things glowering at them. One of the men raised his rifle and then suddenly saw that the creatures had hands.'

'They were human children?'

'They had been born human, Mary. A boy and a girl of about twelve years old, but I don't think one could say much more than that. They died after a few months in captivity, but a thorough study was made of them.

'Yes, I remember that it made rather unpleasant reading. The mental changes were understandable, of course: a craving for raw meat, nocturnal habits, extreme ferocity and terror of man. But there were physical alterations as well. Through running on all fours, the feet had not developed and enormous callouses took the places of knees, while, as a protection against the play bites of the wolves, their bodies had become abnormally hairy. Sexual development had not only come earlier, but followed the normal animal cycle. The girl, for instance, had strong urges during menstruation, and would bay at night to attract the dogs around the mission.

'Does that answer your question?'

'Very well indeed.' Mott nodded. 'And, if these creatures had survived among the wolves and mated with each other, what would their offspring have been like?'

'It's impossible to say, as no cases have ever been recorded, but I think it's obvious that even greater alterations would take place. Though I don't like the word "mutation" since it became popular, it's probably the only one that fits.'

'Good. We're agreed so far, then.' Mott came back to the table and opened his brief-case. 'You admit the possibility of telepathy by means of electrical impulses from the brain. You also admit that a creature placed in an abnormal environment will alter and adapt itself to the new conditions. The wolf-child develops callouses on the knees and an abnormal hairiness. A blind man's senses of touch and hearing are much more acute than an ordinary person's.' He drew a wad of typescript from the brief-case and sat down.

'This is a history of Dunstonholme and the surrounding district, written by David Ainger. I won't bother to tell you how I got hold of it, but it is very carefully compiled and most of his references have been checked. When I read the conclusions he draws in the final chapter, I thought he must have been mad. Now, I almost wish that he had been.' Mott's hand shook slightly as he turned the pages.

'Ainger starts his story with the bombing of the American ship during the war and works backwards. It appears that something happened to, or was done by Frank Jessop that night, but he doesn't tell us what it is. He merely says that the events started him off on his researches.

'In the next chapter he goes into great detail about the failure of the railway project, and the lead mine which was closed down. In both cases the employers did their best to explain the labour troubles as the result of radical agitation, but it is quite clear that at times there was violence and blind panic among the work people.' Mott got up again and paced across the room with the typescript in his hand.

'And so Ainger works back. Back to that chap, Pounder, who was supposed to have been killed by a flock of sheep, and dozens of other events which he got from old diaries, and parish records and folk tales handed down by word of mouth. A quarryman who went mad and threw himself over a cliff – a woman who was stoned to death as a witch, merely because, like Pounder, she wanted to live alone on the moors – stories of demons walking the heather, and a thing called the Draken Worm that comes out of the sea at night. Right back to 1300 and the Children of Paul.' He paused and looked at Mary. 'What do you know about them, my dear?'

'Very little, I'm afraid. So much of the story seems to be just legend. They were religious fanatics, typical of the Middle Ages, followers of a monk who had been expelled from his order. He taught that the rest of humanity was corrupt, and his followers must withdraw from the world if they hoped to gain salvation in the next. One of the Feyne Islands was chosen as their retreat, and they were drowned on their way out to it. That's about all I know.'

'Yes, that's about all that most people know. Ainger has a lot
to say about them and, though I agree with his final conclusions,
the reasons he gives for what happened are quite wrong. He talks
about some impersonal force of evil which has hung over the
area since pre-Christian times, and considers that the Children of
Paul had been infected by it and driven mad.' Mott laid down the
typescript and pulled out his notebook.

'Oh, he was right about their being driven mad, but I think
that happened long before they reached Dunstonholme. I've read
a little about Paul of Ely, or the Young Man from Ely, as he was
sometimes called, and he appears to have been a very rum character indeed: partly a man of science who anticipated Copernicus by
stating that the earth was not the centre of the universe, and partly
a typical religious fanatic of the period. After he was expelled from
his order, the fanatic appears to have taken over. He collected a
large body of disciples and told them that humanity was corrupt
and tainted and they were to withdraw from the world till the last
day when they would be called upon to assist in the judgement of
mankind. Rather like a present-day sect, in fact.'

'I suppose you mean the Exclusive Brethren.' Tom felt sudden
irritation. 'Possibly, but what exactly are you getting at? Just now,
you said that you knew the cause of these . . .'

'Of these disturbances. Yes, I think I do, but please bear with me
a little longer. The story goes that Paul and his followers came here
on their way to one of the islands and, maddened by the Franklin's
refusal of boats, massacred all the villagers and the castle garrison.

'Now, does that seem likely to you? Paul of Ely may have been
a religious maniac, but he certainly was not a fool. The outermost
Feyne is only twelve miles from the mainland. He must have known
that ships would have been sent out against him, as soon as the
authorities heard what he had done. Remember that Edward I, the
"Hammer of the Scots", was on the throne at the time. He wasn't
the man to let a thing like that go unavenged.

'No, I think there was quite a different reason for the massacre: a
much more logical one.' Once again Mott stared out of the window.
Three fishing vessels were entering the bay, pitching slightly as they
crossed the bar.

'It is clear to me that the villagers were killed simply because these people didn't want anybody left to say where they had gone. I am also sure that their hiding place would not have been on one of the islands.' He turned to Tom and nodded.

'Yes, you'll probably say that I'm crazy, but there just isn't any other explanation for the things that have happened. I honestly believe that the Children of Paul, or rather their descendants, are still alive.'

'No, no, no, I refuse to accept that.' Ten minutes had passed since Mott delivered his bomb-shell, and Tom's fingers beat on the table.

'You suggest that those people have existed in the caves since the beginning of the fourteenth century. Over six and a half hundred years! It's impossible. What about food, light, clothing?' He stared around the room, hoping to reassure himself by the sight of familiar objects. The Japanese prints that he had given Mary for a wedding present, the polished Davy lamp, and the French repeating clock which had belonged to his grandmother. Mott's theory was hideous.

And yet, there had been another similar case. Sawney Beane, the Scottish hedger who had hidden with his wife in a cave during the sixteenth century. They had reverted to cannibalism, waylaying travellers by night, and remained undetected for years. Their victims were said to have numbered almost a thousand. When they were at last discovered, their offspring were so numerous that the king himself had led an army against them, and twenty-seven men and twenty-one women, all the products of incest, had been tortured to death in Leith.

No, that was not a fair comparison. Apart from the fact that they killed for human flesh instead of money, the Beane family were simple brigands, and they came out of their cave at night. What Mott suggested was quite different: creatures which had remained underground for over six hundred years.

And yet – and yet. The word kept impinging on his thoughts, as it had done to Mott in the library.

Food might not have been such a difficulty. Some of those limestone systems were enormous, and there could easily be a lake with fish and fresh-water mussels; lichen and edible fungus, too.

Light? All that part of the moor was riddled with crevasses and some shafts might run straight down into the earth, allowing them a glimpse of the sky.

Clothing? There was no problem there. Mott had said that the caves maintained a standard temperature, and he'd answered the question himself when he spoke of the abnormal hairiness of the wolf-children.

It was still crazy, though; still impossible. Six hundred and sixty-six years! Say twenty generations at the most conservative reckoning. Living under such conditions, and inbreeding, they must have degenerated completely.

But so what? Given the tenacity of religious mania – granted that a few of them survived for a couple of generations, the genes would have started to alter and the organism adapt itself to its environment, developing enormous powers of resistance.

Developing other powers as well. As the body changed, Nature might compensate by providing it with a different means of communication and defence. Tom tried to imagine what conditions would be like down there. A little pin-point of light coming down a shaft, dripping rock walls, no change of temperature, no change of seasons, and things descended from men and women waiting: waiting and praying for the last day when the judge would appear and they, the Chosen, would come forth to assist in the punishment of mankind.

Frightened things too, probably. They believed that all the rest of humanity were enemies who would contaminate and destroy them. So, whenever they felt themselves threatened – a quarryman's blast, a bomb exploding, a wreck blowing up – their fear and hatred would rush out like a current of destruction.

Yes, granting that the theory of electric waves from the brain transmitting emotion was tenable – granting that the beings had changed and mutated over the centuries, that could explain everything. Tom heard the front-door bell ring, but he hardly saw Mary get up to answer it.

Various metallic strata in the rock might conduct the impulses, or more probably water. Bates had been standing beside Milkwell Burn when he let go of Keith's chair and had his vision from God. There was a spring in Frank Jessop's paddock. Anything might do it, and it was far too early to consider technicalities. He looked up with a jerk as Mary came back into the room and handed him an envelope.

'It's from Professor Jarrold at the University Research Department. Michael Byrne who lives down the street is one of his students and he asked him to give it to you.'

'Thanks. Yes, this may tell us a little more. It'll be about that hair specimen I sent them.' Tom put on his glasses to read the tiny cramped writing.

My dear Allen,

I am writing to you personally, because I have no desire for my secretary to see what I have to say. I must, of course, compliment you on your skill in micro-surgery, but also point out that this department has little time to enjoy practical jokes. [Tom broke off, frowning. What on earth was Jarrold driving at?]

The enclosed specimen was subjected to a thorough analysis, as you asked. In fact, two of my senior assistants spent a whole morning doing this. They were unable to identify the animal to which the hair belonged, but an examination of the skin tissue revealed an enclosed particle of dead pus, which showed the specimen to be a man-made hoax – an extremely clever one, I admit. But in future, I would be glad if you would confine your humorous activities to persons outside this department.

According to isotope and carbon 5 tests . . . [The paper suddenly seemed to blur before Tom's eyes.] . . . the pus showed that the creature which produced it could not have been less than three hundred years old.

CHAPTER THIRTEEN

The head office of Tyneport Chemical Industries was a brand new building, largely constructed of glass, and decorated in the most modern manner. Huge abstract paintings hung in the reception hall, fountains played before the lift shafts, and snow-white carpets lined the white marble corridors. With the exception of one room, the whole place had an overpowering stench of Notawiff, the firm's best-selling domestic air-freshener.

The exception was the room which belonged to the vice-chairman, Admiral the Hon. George Fetherstone Chadwick Vane, who had transported his furnishings there after the old offices were closed, and imagined himself to be very comfortable indeed. There were no abstracts for him, no carpet, and no air-freshener. Photographs of warships and naval officers covered the walls, the floor was oak, scoured like a quarter-deck, and the atmosphere a pleasant mingling of cigar smoke, whisky, and leather-bound books.

'No, I'm extremely sorry, gentlemen. There may be more things in heaven and earth, but this is a bit too much to swallow.' Admiral Vane had two faces: his own which was usually affable and breezy, and another, morose, glowering and hostile which he had modelled on that of his boyhood hero, Lord Fisher. At the moment, Fisher was very much to the fore. Heavy and flushed, thick lips drawn back and eyes slitted in a scowl, he glared at Tom and Mott.

'Yes, far too much. Naturally I've read about those disturbances at Dunstonholme: there's hardly anything else in the papers nowadays. But I ask you! Chaps who have been living in the caves since the fourteenth century! Telepathic powers that drive people insane! A specimen of tissue that is over three hundred years old!' He snorted loudly as Tom tried to interrupt.

'Oh, I'd like to give you credit of course. We've been friends for some time, Allen, and I suppose I owe my life to you.' Three years previously, the Dunstonholme branch of the Old Comrades Association had held a celebration to mark the twentieth anniversary of Italy's surrender, with Vane as their guest of honour. After knocking back several pints of warm, gassy bitter beer, he had been suddenly smitten by a prostate gland stoppage, and only Tom's speedy arrival had saved him.

'I know about you too, Mr. Mott. Read one of your books, as it happens. About a trip up the Amazon. I didn't think it was at all bad in places.'

'Thank you.' Mott was beginning to dislike the admiral. He had given him what he imagined to be a hair-raising account of the dangers involved, and Tom had followed with a lecture on the scientific importance of the discovery. Both of them appeared to have left him unmoved.

'Not at all. Credit where it's due, and all that.' Vane gave him a stiff bow. A tiny, but irremovable piece of bomb splinter had been lodged in his neck when the R.A.F. mistook his light cruiser for a German battleship in '42.

'I want to make it quite clear that I don't doubt your words or your good faith. It's just that I can't believe the story. Since thirteen hundred, you tell me. No, there may be more things in heaven and earth, as I've said before, but that's too much to swallow.' Vane fiddled with a heavy ebony ruler on his desk.

'And, in any case, assuming that these people really do exist, why come to me about it? Why didn't you go straight to the authorities; the police for example?'

'Three reasons, Admiral.' Tom leaned forward, studying him. Though their earlier arguments had failed, there might be a way to impress his business sense. 'In the first place, the authorities would probably not listen to us till it is too late. Secondly, you have the means to help us. Finally, you may be able to make a great deal of money for your shareholders.'

'Money?' Vane frowned, but there was a sudden interest in his eyes. Tyneport Chemicals had had a lean year, and he wasn't looking forward to the next general meeting. 'Why do you say that?'

'Surely it's obvious, sir. The skin and hair sample was shown to belong to a creature over three hundred years old.' Tom slid the report across the desk. 'Somehow those things have attained the means of enormous longevity, probably to do with diet, I should imagine. Some substance that prevents the hardening of the arteries: raw fish, lichen, edible fungus. Aldous Huxley wasn't the only person who considered the possibility of uncooked carp guts having that effect. A Chinese scholar said the same thing in the fourth century, B.C.

'If we did discover what the cause was, and you patented the substance . . .'

'We'd have every old buster in the world saving up to buy it.'

Vane stopped playing with the ruler and grinned. 'That's quite a point, isn't it? The Voronoff Clinic would close down overnight, and we'd have half our rivals out of business.

'Yes, that really is a point.' His face gleamed with cupidity. 'I'm just a figure-head here, of course. Shareholders like to have a bit of top brass on the board. But I can imagine the killing we'd make, if we came up with a rejuvenator that really worked.

'But what about your second reason? How do you think I can help?' Lord Fisher's glowering expression had vanished, and there was nothing except good-humoured interest in Vane's face. He pushed a box across to them. 'Do help yourselves, gentlemen.'

'Thank you.' Mott sniffed his cigar appreciatively and cut the end. 'These people – or creatures – in the cave have proved themselves to be extremely dangerous, and will become much more so, as I shall tell you later. They have to be rendered harmless, but they must not be killed or injured, as they are obviously of the greatest scientific interest, and financial profit.' He waved the cigar to accentuate the last point.

'You are one of the few persons who can help us because this company has been working on a tranquillizing gas called Psymiac C.'

'Psymiac D, actually. But how on earth did you hear about it, Mr. Mott? It's for the army, and we're supposed to regard it as top secret.' Vane's voice was slightly guarded, but only slightly.

'What! You got it from me, Allen, at the Sandersons' cocktail party.' He frowned, as Tom answered. 'I must have been tight. Get tight pretty often these days, I'm sorry to say, but I've got a damned good reason for it, as you probably know.' He looked at Tom for sympathy.

'Between these four walls, Dorothy has been behaving atrociously of late; quite atrociously.'

'I'm very sorry about that, Admiral.' Tom really did feel sympathetic, for he had heard a good deal about the activities of Lady Chadwick Vane. After a slight concussion following a hunting accident, she had experienced a religious and moral conversion, and now busied herself with good works. Part of the admiral's house had been turned into a home for unmarried mothers, and she had once publicly rebuked him for eating steak while thousands were starving in India.

'Yes, I'm sure you are, my boy.' Vane dragged gloomily at his cigar. 'I've nothing against religion, of course. Excellent thing in its time and place. But, in my opinion, the time and place are an hour in church on Sunday, not a constant barrage every moment of the day.

'But what do you mean about the Psymiac? I shouldn't have mentioned it, of course, but it doesn't really matter. Every major nation has been working on the same lines, and most of them have been far more successful than us. Our chaps have been so mucked about by Whitehall Jacks in Office trying to justify their jobs, that they are still in the experimental stages. Probably be called Psymiac Z before they're finished.' He chuckled at his own wit.

'How does it work, Admiral?'

'Well, the idea is very simple really. I won't bore you with the technical details – I couldn't, even if I wanted to – but the aim is to produce a substance which is harmless, but will render the victim virtually intoxicated. Under its influence, the victim becomes obsessed with one object, and is unable to consider anything else; rather like a very young child, in fact.' Vane was clearly quoting from some lecture or pamphlet.

'He is also tranquil and deprived of concentration. Though entirely preoccupied with the object he is unable to understand how it functions, or to use it. Should the object be a weapon, for instance, he will play with it, but be incapable of putting it to its proper purpose.'

'But, my dear sir, don't you see that that's exactly what we need?' Mott beamed at him. 'If those creatures can be deprived of concentration long enough for us to get them out, there will be nothing to worry about. You have some in your store house, I suppose?'

'Of course we have. Over a hundred cylinders, but you're surely not suggesting that I hand them over to you.' The Admiral's face darkened slightly. 'If those chaps really do exist, I can see the importance of rendering them harmless, but that gas is government property and there'd be the hell of a row if we let it out of our hands.'

'Besides, this batch is just in the experimental stages, and probably very dangerous indeed. We know that the tranquillizing effects work all right, but from tests with animals, it appears that it may be too powerful for the human body to absorb without great risk. If you popped a cylinder or two into those caves you might kill some of them.'

'That's a chance we have to take. Even if we wipe out the whole lot, we've got to do it.' Mott turned to Tom. He had no doubt now that he could persuade Vane to do what he wanted, but Tom's humanitarian feelings were quite a different matter.

'No, you've given me your views, Tom, but we must be realistic. We know very little about those creatures, but we do know something of their powers: thought waves from the brain that can drive men mad. If those waves are effective through the insulation of the earth, what do you imagine they could do on the surface?

'We also know quite a bit about their original nature. The Children of Paul withdrew from the world, because they hated the rest of humanity which they considered tainted and evil. I don't think time will have done anything to decrease that hatred, and they are now waiting for the Day of Judgment, when they will come forth and assist in the destruction of mankind.'

'The Day of Judgment.' The admiral gave another loud snort of contempt. 'When the cows come home. Look, Mr. Mott. Much against my better sense, I'm going to give you the benefit of the doubt. I'll presume that those beings do exist in the caves, and that they are as hostile and dangerous as you say.

'Now, what I suggest, is this. I'll play along with you, but only when I'm ready. After the recent ructions at Dunstonholme, nobody will go up to those moors in a hurry, and there will be very little danger. All we have to do is to wait till our lab boys turn out a reliable batch of Psymiac, and I'll see that a few cylinders don't go on the government inventory. From the last report, I gather we won't have to wait very long. Probably only till the end of next month. After all, the chaps have been down there for over six hundred years. A few weeks won't make any difference.'

'A few days may make all the difference, Admiral Vane. You see, if there is a direct shaft into their caves, they would be able to record the passage of time.' Mott leaned back in his chair, trying to picture it. A tiny pinpoint of light at the top of a tunnel, and dim eyes watching. Morning and night – weeks and months and years – a hundred years – half a thousand years. Deformed hands lifting a stone and scratching marks on the rock walls. The lines of scratches building up over the centuries and running towards the longed-for day of triumph when their judge would reveal himself and mankind be destroyed.

'Could they record time?' Vane raised his eyebrows. 'I don't agree with that. They went down there at the beginning of the fourteenth century, and the calendar wasn't revised by Pope Gregory till the middle of the sixteenth.'

'Quite true, but if they disregarded years and concentrated on one single day, it's possible. As you of course know, the sun's passage varies consistently, and this Paul of Ely appears to have been a man far in advance of his period. He could have contrived a mechanical means of recording time – a marked slab at the foot of the shaft, perhaps, with dimensions depending on its distance from the surface and the angle of the aperture through which the light falls. The light spot would be farthest from a given point at noon each day, and the "noon point" would move backwards and forwards across the scale as the seasons changed, reaching a certain value on Midsummer's Day. All they would need to do is record those values.'

'But again, so what?' The admiral pointed his cigar at Mott like a pistol. 'You said the Day of Judgment which means never. Let's just bide our time till a really reliable batch of gas is available.'

'No, sir, though I would like to agree with you, we can't wait. There is no time, you see.' Mott turned the desk calendar towards Vane. 'Today's date is the twenty-first of June.'

'The British Museum library has a fifteenth-century manuscript which recounts some of the teachings of Paul of Ely. According to its author, he prophesied that the end of the world would take place on Midsummer's Day, nineteen hundred and sixty-six.'

'Well, that's the lot, gentlemen. We've all had time to think it over, and we are all agreed.' Admiral Vane stood at the end of his dining-room table. Behind him hung a large oil painting of himself in full uniform with a telescope under his arm. Now and again it shook slightly and through the wall came the sound of music and sudden peals of laughter. Apparently the unmarried mothers and their offspring were holding a party in the next room.

'We commence the operation at six o'clock on the morning of the twenty-third.' Vane beamed at the group of men in front of him. With the exception of Tom and Mott they were all old friends and comrades.

Commander Rattray who had served with him as a midshipman, and was now the transport manager of Tyneport Chemicals; Leading Seaman Clegg, his chauffeur and general factotum; Chief Petty Officer 'Tubby' Jackson who had been with him when Coastal Command bombed *Athene*, and was in charge of the firm's security. Marine Sergeant Barrat, and Stoker Rose, former heavyweight champions of Chatham and Portsmouth whose bulging, much-decorated chests gleamed alternately behind the reception desk. Men he had commanded in peace and war and almost regarded as brothers.

'Though the whole business is problematic, to say the least, we're going to give our friends here the benefit of the doubt. If these creatures do exist, we'll deal with them.' He smiled at Tom, and then scowled as something thudded against the wall.

'Sorry about that, gentlemen. Undisciplined lot of bitches! Unless my wife learns to control them properly, I'm giving her an ultimatum. Either they go, or I go.

'Now, let's just run through the details again and make sure that everybody knows his job. Transport?'

'It'll be laid on, sir.' Rattray consulted his notes. 'One of our own ten-tonners will take the cylinders to the Dunstonholme side road, and I'll hire a track-laying vehicle for the trip across the moors. Clegg and I will drive, with Barrat and Rose to help us transfer the load.

'I've already started assembling the equipment we need, gas-masks, lamps, a light winch and so on.'

'Good. Then one hour after the gas has been administered, a party of five led by Mr. Mott will enter the caves. I gather that you have accommodation for these horrors, Doctor, should we manage to bring them to the surface?'

'Yes, the old isolation hospital near Denesford. It hasn't been used since the smallpox scare three years ago, and there will be no difficulty. We'll take them there, and then inform the authorities.'

'Excellent. Now, about getting the cylinders from our own warehouse. You'll see that the watchman is conveniently called away, Chief Petty Officer?'

'I'll do that, Admiral, since you order it, but once again I must register my personal disapproval.' Jackson was a red-haired Scotsman with a gammy leg and a mournful expression. 'I know that Mr. Mott and Dr. Allen have told us that there is no time, but in my opinion we should have informed the authorities and let them take whatever action they think fit.

'I must also point out that those cylinders are the property of the Ministry of Defence and can only be removed with their official permission.'

'Damn the Ministry of Defence.' Vane scowled at him. 'Don't you realize that by the time officialdom paid any attention to us, those jokers could be half-way to London? You really are becoming a misery in your old age, Tubby. Nobody would believe that you'd once taken a one-man sub into Mandersfiord.'

'Well, that's about the lot, I think, and it only remains for us to toast the success of our mission.' The admiral felt an enormous sense of excitement as he raised his glass. Apart from the fun of it, this business might give Tyneport Chemicals the biggest killing of all time.

'Please don't get up, gentlemen.' They swung around as the door opened. Lady Vane had once been regarded as a smart woman, but today she was dressed in a sacklike overall and didn't look as though she had visited her hairdresser for weeks.

'I'm so sorry to disturb you, George, but little Lucille Spink thinks she left her doll in here.' Vane's feeling of excitement was replaced by deep shame as she walked across the room. Dorothy had been very strange since her accident, but he'd never imagined she would stoop to that. Her expression told him that she had been listening at the keyhole and had heard every word that was said.

CHAPTER FOURTEEN

'You were right to come to me, Lady Chadwick Vane; quite right.' The Bishop of Welcott came back into his study and sat down facing her. He was dressed in a cassock, having recently laid the foundation stone of a comprehensive school, and he made a fine imposing figure with the light glinting on the purple silk and the silver crucifix on his chest.

'I must apologize for keeping you waiting so long, but it was necessary that I consulted some expert opinions.' After she had given him her information, Dr. Fenge had spent almost an hour on the telephone. He had many contacts and had spoken to Professor Komroff in Warsaw, a reader in Medieval History at London University, and a Harley Street doctor who specialized in geriatrics. He had been very sceptical at first, but each of them had helped him to change his mind.

'Yes, it was your duty to tell me what you happened to overhear. The admiral is your husband, but I am your father in Christ.

'But why didn't he mention it to you himself, I wonder? Surely you should be the first person he would confide in?'

'He tells me nothing, my lord.' Lady Vane gave a small bitter smile. 'George and I have drawn very far apart recently. Since you and Father Morlock helped me so much after my accident, I have been trying to do the same for him, to show him the emptiness and selfishness of his life. I think he resents it bitterly.'

'My poor soul, my poor dear soul.' The bishop's beautifully manicured hand reached out and squeezed hers. 'Though truth has its own wonderful rewards, the upholding of it is sometimes very hard.

'But the admiral appeared quite convinced that Mott's story was true, and these people really do exist?' Once again he took Ainger's typescript from the table and flicked it open at the last chapter.

'I am not entirely certain about that, my lord, but at any rate he was prepared to act on what Mott and Dr. Allen told him.'

'Quite so.' Fenge nodded as he stared at the pages. Could it be possible? he thought. Could those people have managed to live for almost seven hundred years without ever coming out into the light of day? Could those telepathic powers have been developed as the body altered? Could they have maintained their fanatical beliefs till the present? As he thought about it, and remembered what he had heard on the telephone, his remaining doubts started to fade and be replaced by a number of pleasant pictures. Press conferences with himself in the chair; books on the subject; television interviews, newspaper articles, lecture tours all over the world. He might well be a laughing stock, if the whole thing turned out to be a hoax, but the possible glory far outweighed the risk. Besides, though Mott and Vane were objectionable men, they were not fools. If they were prepared to believe, why shouldn't he?

'And you say that this gas they intend to use is a trial batch that has not even been properly tested, Lady Vane?'

'Yes, my lord. That is the main reason why I came to you. During experiments with mice, some of the animals died. It might be murder if they used it on human beings.'

'Of course it would be. Plain murder.' The arrogance of the men, he thought. He'd always disliked the admiral, and Mott had made a most unfavourable impression on him the other day. A chat with a friend who read his books had confirmed it. The fellow was a blustering bully who boasted of his brutalities in print. Well, Mr. Mott was going to have his goose cooked in the very near future. 'I intend to put a stop to it, Lady Vane.'

'My lord, may I speak for a moment.' The bishop's chaplain leaned forward from the sofa. 'If those creatures exist, and are as powerful and inimical as Ainger suggests, there may be very grave dangers involved.'

'Creatures, Toby?' Dr. Fenge frowned sadly at him. 'What a terrible word for a priest to use, Father Morlock. These are men and women, Father. A little different from us, a little strange perhaps, but still fellow human beings; still our brothers.' The opening lines of a sermon started to click into shape.

'Yes, our brothers, Toby: our brothers from the dark. We may pity them for their ignorance, their lack of science and social progress, but can you help admiring them? For six hundred years they have hidden in those caves with only one hope and one aim: that they may keep themselves pure for the arrival of the judge – for the second coming of their master.

'Think of it, Toby. Think of the conditions they have lived under. Try to imagine the cold, and the darkness, and the slime of the pit. Picture them gazing up through some narrow shaft, longing to climb out into God's pure sunlight, but knowing that it was ordained for them to stay there till the appointed time. Can you do anything except envy them their faith?'

'I suppose not, my lord. At the same time, there does seem to be a great element of danger. If these people are in the caves, and I'm afraid I'm still not entirely convinced about that, we should be very careful how we deal with them. These thought waves, or cerebral impulses, or whatever they are, are known to kill, and they did withdraw from the world because they hated humanity. Just who are they waiting for, I wonder? Are they perhaps completely evil and it is not Christ but . . .' He broke off before the bishop's frown.

'But the Devil, Father? Please do not use that name, or the word "evil" to me again. There is no such thing as an evil human being. People are stupid and sick and unaware, but the conception of evil is a myth, a hangover from reactionary thought.

'Oh, I am not claiming that these people will be normal. How could they be after such an entombment? And who knows what terrible persecutions persuaded them to flee from the rest of mankind? Could you have resisted the intolerance of the medieval church, Father Morlock? Could you have faced the Inquisition?'

'Probably not, my lord.' Toby would have liked to point out that the Children of Paul had preceded the English Inquisition by several hundred years, but courage was not his strongest suit.

'Of course you couldn't, and neither could I.' His lordship's smile was a wonderful study of humility. 'Our friends are frightened. That is why they have done these things and developed their terrible power of self-defence.

'So, we must reassure them, Toby. We must prove that there is nothing to be frightened of any more. When they come out into the daylight, we must show them our love and our sense of brotherhood. We must open our arms and cry, "Welcome, comrades. Welcome, dear brothers from the dark."

'And this man Mott – this brutal hooligan would like to gas them like rats.' His smile changed to the expression of outrage which he usually reserved for the Government of South Africa.

'Men and women, and little children too, probably, and he and your husband would destroy them. I shall stop it, Lady Vane. I shall show this Mott up for the brute he is.' There had been an excellent lunch following the foundation stone ceremony, and a bottle of Trois Soeurs and several glasses of brandy spurred his eloquence and drove out all remaining doubts.

'Yes, I'm convinced that old Dave Ainger was right, though his anxieties were groundless. These poor souls do exist, and it is up to us to help them, to calm their suspicion and terror of mankind and give them reassurance. When the morning of Midsummer dawns, I shall be up on the moors waiting to welcome them.

'The land is church property, isn't it, Toby?'

'Oh yes, my lord. It was bought from Lady Railley, just after the First World War. But I really must impress on your lordship that we may be . . .'

'Running into great danger, Father? You may well be right, but I shall still be there. I will go alone, if nobody has the courage to accompany me, and I shall raise my crosier – my simple shepherd's crook, to those poor lost sheep, saying, "Welcome, brothers. Welcome back into the joys of light."

'And now to business, Lady Vane. Now to put a stop to Mott and your husband's intended massacre.' Dr. Fenge got up and pressed the switch of an intercom on his desk.

'Mrs. Ford, will you try and get me the Prime Minister on his private line. After that contact Mr. Wise of the *Tynecastle Echo*, and John Benson of Northern Television. Apologize for the short notice, but say that, if they care to dine with me this evening, I will give them a most interesting news item.

'What's that?' He frowned at his secretary's query. 'Yes, of course they should dress, Mrs. Ford, black tie naturally.' Outside, the cathedral clock started to strike and Fenge looked at his watch. In approximately thirty-six hours' time, the rising sun would bring in Midsummer's Day.

CHAPTER FIFTEEN

'Somewhere within this circumference there must be a shaft leading directly into the caves, possibly several.'

Mott drew a circle on the big survey map which he had pinned to the table. Together with the collection of ropes, gas-masks and torches that Commander Rattray had delivered the previous evening, it made the Allens' dining-room look like the store house for some commando operation.

'Yes, unless we are wrong in every single conjecture, there is bound to be such a shaft. Those people must have explored the caves thoroughly before settling in them, and a direct view of the sky was essential for their purpose. Most probably the entrance will be concealed by a cairn or a pile of boulders, but we'll find it all right.

'Everything is going to go like clockwork, my dear.' He grinned at Mary. 'Admiral Vane has promised us enough gas to tranquillize the population of London, and with all his chaps to help, it should be as easy as falling off a log.'

'But where is the admiral?' Tom consulted his watch. 'He said he would be here at six forty-five and it's almost seven now.'

'Oh, don't worry about Vane. He'll be along all right. A very decent old boy, once you get to know him, and he's entered right into the spirit of the thing.' Mott bent over the map again.

'We transfer the load on to the track-laying vehicle here, and follow the route of those poor kids, Millar and West, across the moor.' Mott intersected his circle with a series of crosses.

'The cylinders only weigh fifty-five pounds apiece, so each of us can carry one. We spread ourselves out at these points, and work in towards the crags till we find the shaft. Then, voila! Bob is a very close relative indeed. We lower our gas down, and wait exactly one hour before going in after it. The effects of Psymiac last for a little over three, and, as we'll be wearing masks, we can repeat the dose if necessary.

'You're quite sure that the hospital accommodation is all right, Tom?'

'Yes, we've got nothing to worry about as far as that's concerned. It's in such a remote spot, that there isn't even a living-in care-taker.'

'Excellent. Then all we have to do now is to wait for old Vane. But what's the matter, Mary? You don't seem very eager for the chase.'

'I'm not eager at all.' She was staring blankly at the map. 'If you really want to know, I'm scared stiff. We know that these creatures have changed both mentally and physically. How can you be sure that the gas will have any effect on them? Look what they have done in the past: driving people insane – killing them; Bates, Ainger, those boys on the motor-cycles. You may not even get close enough to put in your cylinders.

'You're both treating it so lightly, too. "As easy as falling off a log – Bob's your uncle." Tom, I'm frightened. I don't want a lunatic or a corpse for my husband.' She looked up from the map and they could see tears in her eyes.

'I feel guilty as well. Oh, yes, these creatures are a terrible danger and must be stopped, but they were human beings once. Even if the gas is harmless, it seems so brutal to haul them up to the surface and keep them drugged at the isolation hospital, till you've discovered what makes them tick.

'Darling, even at this point, couldn't we just inform the authori-ties and leave it to them?'

'You know perfectly well that we can't. It would take days, maybe weeks, to persuade them of the danger, and we've got less than twenty-four hours.' Tom looked at the sun over the bay. 'If Mott's hunch is right, they will have made their final scale calcu-lation a year ago and counted each separate sunrise since then. That means that they could be intending to come out at any time after daybreak tomorrow. And, if they are allowed to come out unchecked, all hell could be let loose. Imagine the effect of that thought transference in a crowded street.

'Excuse me, though.' The telephone rang in the next room and he went to answer it.

'Don't worry, my dear. I'll see that nobody comes to any harm.' Mott forced himself to sound hearty and confident, but he didn't feel confident at all. What will they be like? he thought. What on earth will they be like after six hundred years of inbreeding, and living under such conditions? Even with the gas, he dreaded the idea of going down into the caves again, though he would never admit it to Mary. He bent over the map and then turned as Tom came back into the room.

'What's the matter? Something gone wrong? You look as if you had seen a ghost?'

'Yes, something's gone wrong – everything has.' Tom nodded as he came slowly towards them. 'That was Admiral Vane. He's not coming.'

'What!' The pencil snapped between Mott's fingers. 'And why the hell not? He gave me his word that he'd be here. What about the rest of 'em; the chaps with the lorry carrying the cylinders?'

'Nobody is coming. It's all over and there's no gas available. It appears that the authorities got wind of our plans and stepped in.

'All I know for sure is that very early this morning a party of soldiers arrived at the warehouse with authorization from the Ministry of Defence to remove the whole consignment to an Ordnance Corps depot near Scarsdale. The watchman rang up Vane, and he at once contacted the duty officer at North-Eastern Command headquarters, saying that the gas was an untested batch which they needed for further experiments. But it was no good. The orders had been issued by Whitehall and nothing could be done to counteract them.

'I don't think we should blame old Vane. He honestly does seem to have done his best to stop them.'

'I'm not blaming him, Tom. I'm not blaming anybody, except the bastard who tipped off the army.' Mott stared gloomily out of the window. 'All the same, it appears to me that we're sunk; completely and utterly sunk.

'But that's odd.' He frowned as he looked down the street.

'Where have all the cars gone? Come and see for yourself.' The Crown Hotel had very poor parking facilities and the reporters staying there always left their cars in the square overnight. Now, apart from a milkman's trolley, there wasn't a vehicle in sight.

'Yes, it's certainly queer.' Tom followed his gaze. 'There were at least a dozen of them there last night.

'And just what does Barry Maynard think he's doing? He knows he should watch out for that heart of his.' An old man on a bicycle had rounded the bend and was pedalling madly up the slope towards them.

'It looks as though he's on his way here.' Tom hurried to the front door, as the bicycle lurched to a halt, and the local newsagent got off and came staggering up the path.

'Barry, how many times have I got to tell you not to ride that bicycle up-hill?'

'I know I shouldn't, Doctor, but I had to see you at once.' The man was gasping for breath.

'You've got to look at this, sir. You've got to tell me that it can't be true; that somebody's gone barmy, or is playing a joke on us.' He clutched a rolled newspaper in his right hand.

'Gave me the turn of my life it did, when I opened the bundle just now. I thought my eyes must be packing up.' Maynard steadied himself against the doorpost. 'I couldn't send the boys out with 'em, Doctor. Not till I'd spoken to somebody, and the wife said you was the best person, now that Father Ainger has gone.

'It surely can't be true, can it, Doctor Allen?'

'We'll tell you that when we've seen what you're talking about, Mr. Maynard.' Mott reached past Tom and took the paper from him, unrolling it slowly, and dreading what he expected to find; another tragedy, more deaths, more people driven out of their minds. As the front page came into view, he knew that reality far exceeded his imaginings. The headlines were two inches deep and below them was a picture of Dr. Fenge. THE DUNSTONHOLME OCCURRENCES . . . THE BISHOP BREAKS HIS SILENCE . . . IS THIS THE TRUE REASON?

'The fool,' he muttered, as he started to read the column. 'God, the stupid, conceited, murderous fool! "In an exclusive interview with our editor and the chairman of Northern Television last night, Dr. Russell Fenge, Lord Bishop of Welcott, stated what he believes to be the true cause of the recent events at Dunstonholme . . ." See for yourselves . . .' Mott held out the paper for Tom and Mary. 'A miracle from the fourteenth century – the frightened people of the caves – our brothers returning to us from the Dark Ages. We must welcome them. We must reassure them and calm their fears by the proof of our love and comradeship. All people with courage and goodwill shall join with me on a joyful pilgrimage of welcome . . .'

'And, by this afternoon . . .' Tom stared down at the square. It was quite empty and peaceful now, but in a few hours' time, things would be very different. Cars and buses would have come pouring in from every direction. Crowds would pack every square yard till nightfall, when the bishop proposed to lead them up to the moors on his 'joyful pilgrimage'.

'We must do something. We've got to stop it. There'll be a slaughter out there, unless we do something.' As always the hills looked very lovely in the clear morning light, but Tom could hardly bring himself to look at them. 'Even without the gas, there must be something we can do.'

'Is there? I don't think so.' Mott shook his head. 'The gas was the only possible weapon we had, and without it we are power-less. It also appears that that devil, Fenge, has got the authorities in the palm of his hand. I'll tell you what I'm going to do, however, and I'd strongly advise you to join me.' He nodded towards his car which was parked in the drive.

'In a very short time, every road in the vicinity will be jammed tight with traffic. I intend to pack my bags and get the hell out of this village while the going is good.'

CHAPTER SIXTEEN

'My friends – my dear friends.' Loudspeakers were mounted on his lorry and the bishop's voice rose and fell over the village square. 'We are met here this evening, not merely in the hope of witness-ing one of the most amazing events in history, but as pilgrims united in one thing: our common humanity.' His eyes swept across the crowd and he bowed to a Salvation Army girl.

'We are members of many races and many nations. We have different creeds and beliefs.' It was the turn of a party of Indian students to receive a bow. 'But we are all human beings joined together by love.' There was a ragged cheer from some teenagers by the churchyard, and though Dr. Fenge smiled paternally at them, he was glad of the solid line of police around his lorry.

The crowd really was vast – far, far bigger than he had imagined possible – and he felt a certain trepidation, recalling his telephone conversations of the previous evening. The Prime Minister had been completely sceptical at first, but had become concerned as he heard the facts, and proposed sending troops into the area, in case there was danger. It had taken all Fenge's eloquence to persuade him that the dangers were non-existent before he had decided to co-operate. He had also demanded a personal assurance that the Church Commissioners, who owned the land, would accept full responsibility should anything go wrong.

'Love, my friends. Love that is without fear and forgives every-thing.' He turned towards the television cameras and adopted what a hostile press sometimes called his 'hunted stag expression', chin forward, face held slightly sideways to show off his undoubtedly handsome profile, and eyes gazing soulfully up at the sky.

Yes, it really was quite a crowd. A lot of factories and shops and offices must have been understaffed during the day. His dinner party had paid a heavier dividend than he expected, and half a dozen newspapers had given the story banner headlines. Since early morning, people had been pouring to Dunstonholme in the hundreds, not merely from Tynecastle and the surrounding district, but from all over the country. What he had intended was a select and serious party to join the welcoming committee he had hurriedly collected on the telephone, but the thing had snowballed. There was nothing particularly serious about his audience either. The majority appeared to be mere sensation-seekers, come for 'a bit of a lark', and the hope of viewing a curious spectacle. Already the police had closed the roads to stop more vehicles reaching the village and cordoned off the paths to the moor.

'Soon, those of us who are strong and active enough to make the journey are going up to the hills where we will keep our vigil. We shall wait throughout the night in prayer and hope and meditation. But there will be no trace of fear in our hearts, though there is, of course, some element of risk.' He was about to mention 'this nettle danger', but remembered it had been used by a Tory prime minister.

'These poor distressed people whom we hope to welcome at daybreak are frightened. Also seven centuries ago, our ancestors – yours and mine – persecuted them without mercy. That is why they believed mankind to be evil and withdrew from the world. That is why they have developed, over the centuries, this terrible power of self-defence, the probable nature of which Professor Tonks has so lucidly described to you.' He bowed to a bearded figure on the bench behind him.

'Yes, their thoughts can kill. They have killed in the past, as you know. But I am convinced that they will not harm us when they realize why we have come. Our thoughts, my friends, our thoughts of love and comradeship and brotherhood will go out to those frightened souls and banish their fears.' Another stab of anxiety pierced him as more leather-jacketed teenagers shouldered their way into the square. No real harm in them of course. Just fun-loving youngsters, but they could be difficult. He closed his address by admitting that there was of course no guarantee that the Children of Paul did exist, and that all the available information was based on the researches of 'our late brother, the Reverend David Ainger'.

There were many speakers to follow the bishop, and all of them were important figures in their own lines. First was Sir Robert Blascombe, author of more than sixty books, crusader for a hundred causes, eighty-five years old. He had been brought to Dunstonholme in an ambulance, and would be carried up to the moors in a chair borne by Rover Scouts. His white hair stirred nobly in the breeze, but even the loudspeakers couldn't make his words audible, though a few listeners caught references to peace and the brotherhood of mankind.

Mr. Norbert Trant came next. He was a short bustling American who stated that he was a lecturer at Oxford University, seconded from Harvard, an authority on early English dialects, and the possessor of a completely open mind. 'I want to make it perfectly clear that I am here at the bishop's request, and have no idea at all whether these people do or do not exist. If they emerge, however, I must ask you to keep absolutely silent, so that I may address them in their own tongue.' Mr. Trant paused and looked sternly at the Salvation Army band.

'The message which I have been asked to deliver commences as follows . . .' He cleared his throat, threw back his head and emitted a series of harsh, guttural bellows which drew thunderous applause from the young members of his audience.

Following Mr. Trant, the crowd were entertained by the 'Tynebeat' pop group who gave a spirited rendering of 'One More River to Cross', but there were more speeches to be heard.

A Member of Parliament, a celebrated poet who read a long ode of welcome which he had composed on the train from London, the leader of the pop group to show that youth was well to the fore, a best-selling writer of science fiction, a female economist who had once proved conclusively that the United States would be bankrupt and on the verge of civil war before the end of 1960. All these people had a great deal to say, and at every word the sun sank a little lower behind the hills and the air grew colder. Moonlight was streaming across the bay when the final speaker lifted the microphone.

He was a superintendent of police and the message, which he delivered in a rasping monotone, was quite different from those of his predecessors. Whilst admitting that there had been a number of unexplained events in the neighbourhood during the last few days, he made it quite clear that he personally considered the idea of people living in the caves to be an elaborate hoax for which somebody would be severely punished. He also dwelt long and lovingly on the penalties for civil disturbance.

'When told to do so, those of you wishing to proceed to the moors will line up at the right of the square in an orderly manner. I repeat, *in an orderly manner*.

'I will also repeat what I said earlier. There is an ample force of officers at my disposal, and I have spoken to the Welcott magistrates. They have given me their assurance that any acts of hooliganism will receive the heaviest sentences that the law allows.' He stepped down and gave a curt order to one of his inspectors.

So, they got ready. Sir Robert Blascombe was hoisted on to his chair, the bishop, the poet and Mr. Trant stationed themselves at the head of the procession with the rest of the official party at their heels, and the police started to form the crowd into line. That took some time, but at last everybody was in place. Just after the church clock had struck ten, the superintendent gave another order and the bishop raised his crosier. The Salvation Army band burst into 'The Race that long in Darkness pined have seen a glorious Light,' and they started to march off to keep their vigil.

'Look, Dorothy, we can't associate ourselves with this monkey show.' Though Admiral Vane had little in common with his wife since her conversion, though he knew she had betrayed him, she was his wife, the mother of his children, and they had been very happy in the past. When she had insisted on going to Dunstonholme, he had known that it was his duty to accompany her.

'Either the whole business is a farce, and these creatures do not exist, or there really is terrible danger. Nobody has ever accused me of cowardice, but it's plain madness to go up to those moors.'

'Then don't go, George. Stay here, or get into the car and drive home, if you're frightened. But don't try to stop me.' She pulled her arm away from him.

'Oh, my dear, surely you can trust the word of that good man. You were deceived by Mott and Dr. Allen: you wanted to destroy those poor people. But can't you realize the truth now? They are merely frightened and . . .'

'And will become as meek as lambs as soon as the bishop talks to them.' Vane shook his head. He had the sudden feeling that everything that had happened was part of a bad dream, but the crowd filing out of the square gave him the lie, as did the music.

Another hymn had replaced 'The Race that Once . . .', and the words were clear on the breeze. 'Hark, Hark, my soul! Angelic songs are swelling . . . O'er earth's green fields and ocean's wave-beat shore . . .' The breeze was blowing up now, driving across the moors and rippling the waters of the bay.

'No, I'm quite sure they won't. A group of people who have existed on nothing but hatred for almost seven centuries aren't going to change merely because Fenge asks them to.' Another gust of wind drove the music towards them. 'Angels of Jesus . . . Angels of Light . . . Coming to welcome the Pilgrims of the Night . . .'

'Don't you understand that, Dot? Can't you realize that their whole existence has been based on hatred for the rest of mankind?' Vane remembered what he had read, and seen, and been told. How Colonel Keith's body had looked – the dead madman on the yacht – the knot of obscenely matted hair and Professor Jarrold's letter: 'the creature which produced this could not have been less than three hundred years old.'

'You talk about the love of that crowd flowing out to them, but that's damn nonsense. In my opinion it's nothing but a bunch of lunatics, hooligans, and the kind of curious fool who runs out to witness a street-shooting without a thought that he might receive a bullet himself.

'Oh, I'm sorry, my dear. I shouldn't have said that. It's just . . .' He started to apologize, but she had already turned coldly away and was hurrying to join the tail of the procession. Its front ranks were well out of the village now, and over the crest of the hill above them a belt of cloud was drifting seawards to obscure the moon.

'All right, old girl. You win as usual,' he said. 'I'll come with you. Bloody fool that I am.' Vane grinned slightly at the final verse of the hymn. 'Rest comes at length . . . though Life be long and dreary . . . the Day must break . . . and darksome Night be past . . .'

Yes, the day will break all right, he thought, so let's go and see what it brings. He tightened his coat and walked after her, feeling a certain comfort from the weight of the heavy automatic in his pocket. If anything did go wrong, he intended to add a personal welcome for the Pilgrims of the Night.

'And with the moving spectacle of all those people marching away behind the bishop, we leave Dunstonholme and return to the studio.' Tom smiled miserably at Mary as he switched off the car radio. In a few minutes they would all have committed a serious crime and she would have risked her life.

But what else could they do? They had tried every obvious course and failed each time. He and Mary had called on the Chief Constable of the county and warned him of the dangers involved, while Mott had telephoned a senior official at the Home Office and the editor of a national newspaper. Not one of them had paid the slightest attention. Either the authorities were completely sceptical, or Dr. Fenge held them in his pocket.

Yes, this was the only way. For over six hundred years those beings had waited in the caves, with no art, no science, nothing except hatred and their founder's promise to sustain them. And they believed that at sunrise tomorrow the promise would be fulfilled. The judge would appear and they would come forth to assist him in the destruction of mankind.

They would be wiped out of course. As soon as their nature and their powers were revealed, the authorities would act and they would be destroyed like vermin. But, before that happened, there could be a massacre. The radio had said that over a thousand people were marching up that hillside.

'Here he is.' The two cars were parked in the cutting of a little wood, well out of sight of the road, and Tom opened a rear door, as Mott came silently through the trees. 'Well, any luck? Did you see the cylinders?'

'Yes, they're there all right.' Mott climbed into the car, breathing heavily. Before leaving Dunstonholme, he had filled a paper bag with soot, and his blackened face and hands looked extremely sinister in the moonlight.

'The place is just a small transit depot, and they haven't even bothered to unload the lorry. It's parked quite near the gate too: an open six-wheeler.' He took a flask out of his pocket and pulled deeply at it.

'No, I don't think we're going to have too much difficulty. There will probably be only a dozen men or so under a sergeant, by the look of it. The road is in our favour too. Three hundred yards from the camp gate there's a narrow bend which my old bus should jam pretty effectively.' He wiped the neck of his flask and handed it across to Mary. 'You may need a swig of that, my dear.

'The chaps look pretty much on their toes, so we'll have to do everything exactly as planned. There are two sentries at the gate and another one marching around the fence. They have probably been told to keep an extra special look-out tonight. I don't imagine their rifles will be loaded, but a bayonet is a very unpleasant weapon.

'Now, let's just run through it once more, shall we? Your part first, old boy.'

'Mine's simple enough, isn't it?' Tom looked at the dashboard clock: twenty minutes to midnight, and the sun rose at 4.45.

'As soon as you flash the lorry lights, I follow in your car and leave it immobilized at the bend to block the road. Provided that you manage to get through the gate, there doesn't seem to be any difficulty about that. It's what Mary has to do that worries me.

'I suppose we couldn't change roles?'

'Not a chance of it.' Mott shook his head. 'As I said, those sentries look as though they have been specially alerted, and they'd probably be suspicious of a man. An injured woman though, and a very pretty one, if I may say so, will be quite a different matter. Besides, I'll need you on the lorry, Tom.'

'Don't worry, darling.' Mary squeezed his hand. 'The Rover has safety-belts and a heavy chassis, and I'll only do enough damage to make it look realistic.

'I'm dreading what comes afterwards: when I'm locked in the guard house, without knowing what's happening to you on the moors.'

'Always assuming that we manage to reach the moors.' Mott squinted at the map. 'We're about eighty miles from Dunstonholme, as the crow flies, which makes it over a hundred and fifty by the side roads we'll have to take. I'll be able to cut the telephone wires all right, but they are bound to contact the police before too long, and that big six-wheeler is going to make a pretty conspicuous target. Also, it's doubtful if we'll manage to get up the hill without a track-laying vehicle.

'All the same, let's keep our fingers crossed and hope for the best. Don't forget to bring the masks when you leave the car, Tom, and you start out in exactly ten minutes from now, Mary. Right; the best of luck to all of us.' He climbed out and then suddenly grinned and reached in his pocket.

'But I'm becoming forgetful myself. Your main stage prop, my dear, so lay it on good and strong.' He handed Mary a tube of red paint and then hurried quickly off through the trees.

Staff Sergeant Randle, commanding officer of Scarsdale Transit Depot, was an ageing cantankerous soldier who had long suspected that life was treating him unfairly. The events of the day had turned his suspicions into certainty.

'Yes, sir,' he said into the telephone. 'Yes, Captain, your Orders have been carried out to the letter. At the same time, sir, I must officially ask you for reinforcements. Private Haggard has reported sick with a sprained tendon, and I have only eight effective men under my command. I would also point out, sir, that most of us have been on duty since five o'clock this morning.

'Very well, sir. The extra guard will be maintained till further notice, but I intend to forward a strong protest to the area commander. Goodbye, sir.' He replaced the phone and scowled across at his corporal.

'I don't know, Syd. I don't know what the bleeders think they're up to. For six ruddy months, they stick us out in this God-forsaken hole with nothing to do, and not even a pub within walking distance.

'But today! Blimey, you'd think a bloody war had started or something.' Randle pulled gloomily at his pipe, considering how he had been dragged out of his bunk by a telephone call from H.Q., and ordered to send the lorry to Tynecastle and collect a load of gas cylinders.

He had at once stated that the depot was already bulging with equipment and there was no more storage room, but his objections had been brushed aside. The consignment could remain on the lorry under strong guard till other arrangements were made.

'You can say that again, Sarge.' His second in command nodded in full agreement. He and two men had taken the lorry to the warehouse, and as no civilians were about at that hour to operate a hoist, they had had to load the whole consignment by hand. He had ricked his neck painfully in the process.

'That was Carter again, I suppose?'

'Yes, Captain Bloody Carter, may Hell be hot for him. "I'm not arguing with you, Sergeant, I'm giving you an order." ' Randle attempted to mimic the clipped Sandhurst accent. ' "That special guard will remain on duty, till you hear otherwise." Christ, what does he think we are? The Foreign Legion, or something?'

'I think it's all a trick, Sarge. A try-on to see if we're on our toes, like.' The corporal was still young, but he was beginning to adopt Randle's elderly mournful expression.

'The watchman at the warehouse told us that that gas was an untested lot and no good to us, or anybody else, for that matter. You remember what Carter said after the inspection last month, Sarge? Didn't half let us have it, did he?

'Yes, I think it's all a ruddy trick to see that you keep the lads up to the mark.'

'You could have something there, Syd. It's just the kind of thing that a bastard like Carter would think up.' Randle was due to retire at the end of the year, and he hadn't taken his tiny command at all seriously.

'They want to see if we carry out the orders exactly, and some miserable sod may be snooping on us right now. Let's take a turn round, just in case.' He put on his tunic and marched stiffly out of the room. Captain Carter bore him no love at all and would be delighted if he lost a stripe before December.

'Everything all right, Private Kerr?' Randle returned the sentries' sloppy greeting with quite unaccustomed smartness. 'All quiet?'

'Quiet as the grave, Sarge. It always is. But what's all this about anyway? Can't you let a couple of us turn in now? You've never had more than one bloke on duty before.'

'You'll turn in when you're told to, lad. In the meantime, just keep your eyes open, and stand to attention when you talk to me.' Randle squared his shoulders ostentatiously. At this very moment, one of Carter's spies might be hidden in the wood watching him through a pair of night-glasses. 'I'll see that you get a cup of cocoa before long, though.'

He turned and looked up the road. There was a car coming, which was most unusual at this time of night, since it was just a short loop, only serving the depot and a couple of farms, before rejoining the main motorway to Tynecastle.

It was coming fast too, and being driven damned badly. Yes, it seemed to be lurching from one side of the road to the other, and the fool hadn't even got his headlights turned on. Tight as a tick he must be. Some farmer who had been celebrating a bumper harvest in advance, probably. Randle grinned enviously and then stiffened. The car suddenly rose over the verge, scraped the wire fence which surrounded the camp, and then shot across the road again and fell on its side in the ditch.

'You men, stay here.' It was unlikely that Carter would have gone to such lengths of deception, but Randle still wasn't taking any chances. Every inch a soldier, he waited until the gate was raised for him, before trotting briskly towards the wreck.

No, this was no trick of the captain's. Randle winced as his torch shone through the window. No drunk farmer either. There was a girl sprawled under the steering-wheel – her safety-belt hadn't been fastened – and blood was everywhere: on the seat and the windscreen, and dribbling on to the floor from what looked like a deep gash in her forehead, though he could see that she was still breathing.

'Right, lads. Over here at the double and give me a hand.' He tugged at the inside doors, but they were both locked. 'You go and fetch the first-aid box, Corp.

'Not that way, you fool.' Kerr had raised his rifle butt to break the window. 'Broken glass won't do her cut any good. Lever the door open with your bayonet while I go and ring for an ambulance.'

Poor kid, he thought, as he ran back to the depot. She really had copped a packet. A pretty girl too, rather like his brother's wife, Mavis. She must have been drunk of course, but he took a drop too much himself sometimes, and he wouldn't condemn somebody who might be dying. That cut looked really nasty, and there was a hell of a lot of blood about. He just hoped Kerr pulled her out gently.

'Get some water on the boil, Smith, there's been an accident.'

His off-duty men must have heard the crash and were standing sleepily before their hut. 'Spence and Harmsworth, take over the gate.'

He ran heavily on towards the guard room, but stopped dead as his hand reached the knob of the door. The engine of the parked lorry had suddenly roared into life and the vehicle was starting to move forward.

Though he had become an idle soldier in his later years, Randle was no coward. He had been wounded in Cyprus and decorated in Korea, and under normal circumstances he would have jumped on to the step of the cab and tried to make a fight of it. It was the appearance of the driver that held him back.

'Hideous, it was, gentlemen,' he stated at the subsequent court of inquiry. 'Quite horrible, and as I shone the torch into the cab and saw those great bloodshot eyes glaring at me, I seemed to come all over queer.

'Yes, sir, you can accuse me of cowardice, if you think fit, but I've never liked apes since I was stationed at Gib., and I honestly thought it was a ruddy great gorilla hunched over that steering-wheel.'

CHAPTER SEVENTEEN

Midsummer Day, nineteen hundred and sixty-six. A cold, dark morning with the wind driving across the moors in gusts, and the moon darting in and out of clouds like a small hunted animal.

'Another two and three-quarter hours to sunrise, Dorothy.' The Vanes were crouched in a hollow formed by three boulders, a little behind the rest of the crowd which was spread out in a wide semi-circle. Beyond them the crags of Pounder's Hole stood like monstrous sentinels, stationed to guard the valley. The superintendent's warnings had proved to be quite unnecessary, and the cold and the grimness of the place had soon damped everybody's high spirits. One or two people were pacing about to keep themselves warm, but the majority had found what shelter they could and were sticking to it. Here and there, where tea was being brewed, were the flickers of oil stoves.

'Do have some brandy, my dear. It's bitterly cold.'

'No thank you, George. I want to keep my mind quite clear.' Though she was shivering, Lady Vane shook her head. In the far distance the lights of a southbound train suddenly made her think of warm, holiday things: beaches under the sun, blue seas and the constant murmur of cicadas in the bougainvillaea.

'What do you think they will look like, George? Have you got any clear picture in your head?'

'I've got several unpleasant pictures, but I don't suppose any of them are even remotely accurate. The only concrete evidence we have for their existence is the tuft of hair Tom Allen found in Ainger's hand.

'He must have been quite a boy, old Ainger. He thought he knew what was in those caves, yet he went down there completely alone. That would have taken a hell of a lot of courage.' The admiral felt slightly ashamed of his own anxieties, as he thought of Ainger. Perhaps Tom and Mott had been wrong all the time. After all, if those creatures did exist, they had been human beings once. They couldn't have changed entirely. They couldn't be completely evil. Perhaps the sight of so many people waiting to welcome them really might . . . He looked up as footsteps came towards him.

'Ah, good morning, Lady Vane.' The bishop beamed at them.

'And, good morning to you, Admiral. You decided to join us after all then. Did you have a change of heart perhaps? A sudden feeling that matters cannot be so terrible?' Dr. Fenge looked very snug in fur-lined boots, a duffel-coat and a Russian cap. There was a shining silver crosier in his hand.

'No, my lord, I've had no change of heart. I still have strong doubts that those beings exist, but if they do, I think you may have done a dreadful thing in bringing this crowd up here.' Vane scowled up at him. This man was brave too, he thought, but not like Ainger. His courage came from boundless self-esteem and lack of imagination.

'The only reason I am here is that my wife insisted on coming, and I felt it was my duty to accompany her.'

'Excellent, Admiral. The care of another person is as good a reason as any other.' Dr. Fenge's dentures glinted in the moonlight.

'So, you are still a doubting Thomas, Admiral Vane. You know, it may be presumptuous of me, but I've always felt that Jesus must have loved Thomas the best of all his disciples. The others were supported by a joint faith, but he had to carry his cross of doubt all alone.

'You are admiring my crosier, Lady Vane?' He held it out to her. 'Yes, it is rather beautiful, I think; silver inlaid with gold and purple amethysts. The Archimandrite of Sofia gave it to me when I visited his country last year. A costly possession for a simple priest like myself, but one couldn't refuse a gift from such a good old man.'

'It is very lovely, my lord.' Lady Vane raised her voice in an attempt to conceal the admiral's snorts of annoyance. 'Simple priest' was a strange description for Dr. Fenge, he thought, and he had heard that the 'good old man' was a cold-blooded murderer who owed his position to the secret police.

'And now, I must go and visit the rest of our friends. I want to see that everybody is in the right frame of mind before sunrise.' The bishop bowed and moved away across the heather.

So, the morning crept on. Three o'clock: another train rumbled towards the south, the wind dropped slightly, the clouds thinned, and the landscape appeared to stretch endlessly away beneath the moon. Paul's Point crouched like an animal at the mouth of the bay with the castle behind it, and the village was a glow of light – a lot of lamps had been kept burning in Dunstonholme that night.

Four o'clock: the moon was moving north behind the humps of the border hills, and the valley between the rocks had been obscured by shadow.

Four thirty: in the east there was a hint that the sky was lightening, but the moon was completely hidden. The crowds were beginning to stir now, and people were walking up and down and flapping their arms to keep themselves warm. They were still very subdued, however, and there was hardly any noise.

Four forty-five: the sky slowly turned from deep purple to grey and a rim of scarlet appeared on the sea. The police spread out to form a cordon before the crowd, Sir Robert Blascombe was hoisted on to his chair, and the official party led by the bishop moved nearer to the valley.

Five: a cock crowed in the far distance, and a huge red sun was dragging itself out of the water and flooding the moorland. Everybody stared at the valley with hope and excitement and not a little fear. Everybody watched the little group that was stationed before the crags. Sir Robert's white hair streamed out like a halo in the breeze that had started to blow again, and the bishop's crosier shone gaily in the morning light. It was going to be a lovely day, that at least seemed certain. The sun was already quite high in the sky and sucking up mist from the ground.

Six thirty: bracken and gorse bushes swayed in the wind, but there was no other movement between the rocks, and sections of the crowd were becoming restive. The air was filled with a tinkle of transistor radios and a party of youths were wrestling in the heather. The admiral became tired of holding his binoculars trained on the valley, which no longer appeared hostile and sinister, but warm and friendly in the sunlight.

'Well, Dorothy, if you ask me, nothing is going to happen; nothing at all. I was a fool to have believed the story in the first place. Have a look for yourself.' He felt stiff and cold from his night's vigil, and the climb up to the moors had taxed him severely. As the sun rose, trepidation had changed to annoyance, and his main ambition was to get home and have a hot bath.

'I'll stay here for exactly one more hour, and then I'm off.' He looked at his watch. Well after seven, and the crowd were getting more and more restive and making a lot of noise. Far out at sea a tanker was clawing north against the swell, and a flock of gulls wheeled screaming across the moor.

I should have expected it of course, Vane thought. Even if those creatures did exist, they couldn't have recorded time accurately over more than six centuries. There must have been miscalculations of the noon point, and dark mornings when the sun was obscured by cloud or fog. It was impossible that they could have hit upon one day out of almost a quarter of a million.

Half past seven, and the police would have to take action before long. The bishop and his party still stood patiently before the valley, but now and again a cat-call was shouted at them and a group of youths were performing a slow hand-clap.

'What's that though?' Vane looked up with a jerk. The noise of the crowd had suddenly stopped and been replaced by a whistling, howling sound that didn't come from the valley, but from the right of it where the crags fell away to rejoin the moor.

'Can you see anything, Dorothy?' The sound was much louder now: a screaming agonized howl that might be being made by a soul under some unspeakable torture.

'Yes, yes, I think so.' His wife swung the binoculars across the crags. Behind a clump of gorse bushes, something was moving. Two things which appeared to be crawling on all fours through the bracken, and one of them was making the noise. They crawled on to the end of the gorse, and then very slowly rose to their feet. Two human figures wearing leather jackets, and the leader had a pair of bagpipes strung round his neck. They performed a grotesque war dance for a moment and fled hurriedly as a party of police moved towards them.

'There you are, Bishop. Them's your monsters – Bill and young Ted. Why don't you go after 'em.' The chorus of shouts rose to a cheer as the bagpiper made a neat swerve and two constables rolled heavily down a scree shoot. 'Good lad, Bill. Give us another tune then.'

'Damned young hooligans.' Vane pulled himself to his feet. 'Come on, Dot, let's get out of here. I knew it was bound to end up as a bear garden.' Other people were sharing his views, filing away down the slope, and in the hope of restoring order, the Salvation Army band had burst into action.

> 'Oh, dear Lord, remember me.
> Jesu, friend, remember me.
> Though a sinner, I shall be
> Clean, if thou remember me.'

With cymbals clashing and trombones blaring away, they gave it all they'd got, but the chorus of shouts and cheers still continued.

'Dorothy, what's the matter?' The admiral winced as she grasped his wrist and her nails dug painfully into the flesh. 'You feeling poorly, or something? Caught a chill perhaps?' Her body was trembling and her face flushed, as though by a high fever.

'No, no, I'm all right, but look for yourself, George.' She handed him the glasses. 'For God's sake, look for yourself.'

'Look at what?' He adjusted the binoculars, and stared across at the crags. All he could see at first were the rocks, and the heather, and bracken stirring in the wind. Then something that was not bracken moved, and he understood.

During the last few minutes, everybody had been watching the boys and the police, and nobody had noticed what was happening in front of them. Down the valley, monstrous in the sunlight, came the Children of Paul.

CHAPTER EIGHTEEN

Tom and Mott had been crawling along minor roads in the hope of avoiding the police, but time was running out. They had to take a chance and come into the open. Mott's foot went down on the accelerator as a dual carriageway opened up in front of them. The lorry must have been recently tuned and it shot forward like a bolted horse.

'Watch out, though.' Tom clutched the dashboard for support as they hurtled into the fast lane. He was very tired and desperately worried about Mary. 'If those cylinders come adrift, we won't be much use to anybody.'

'Don't worry about my driving, old boy. I could have turned professional, if life hadn't called me to greater things.'

'Get out of the way, you bastard.' Ignoring the blasts of his horn, a small family saloon attempted to pull out in front of them, but Mott's foot remained wedged on the throttle. With only inches to spare and its off-side wheels bucketing on to the soft verge, the heavy truck thundered past.

'We checked that the cylinders were secure enough, so just relax and leave the rest to me.' Mott squinted at his watch. Almost seven o'clock and the sun was high in the sky. The fuel in the tank had been very low and they had had to go miles out of their way to find a filling station that was open. All the same, the speedometer needle was rigid at sixty-five, and the next roundabout should bring them to the Dunstonholme road. A few miles along it was a cart track that led up to the moors, after that it was anybody's guess what happened. Those boys, Millar and West, had used it, but there was a marked difference between a motor-cycle and a ten-ton lorry, and he had no idea what the surface or the gradients were like.

'The wind is one thing in our favour anyway.' Tom looked at the trees. As Vane had said, they had enough gas to tranquillize the population of London, but if the creatures really did come out, they would have to release it in the right direction.

'Slow down though, can't you? The cylinders may be secure, but they are also damned heavy.' The roundabout was in sight now, with 'Reduce Speed' signs flashing past, but Mott made no move to obey them.

'If one of the ropes snaps, we'll have had it.' He broke off when Mott finally did brake. The truck swung madly towards the roundabout . . . the door handle jammed against his side. As it did so, he heard Mott curse.

The side road to Dunstonholme was closed. At the end of the roundabout was a diversion arrow, and behind the arrow, two police cars were stationed with a constable standing between them. He obviously hadn't heard about the stolen lorry, and merely waved them to the left. Probably the village had become completely jammed with traffic and they had been forced to seal it off.

'Blast the fellow's eyes.' Mott changed into a lower gear and accelerated again, aiming straight for the policeman. There was room enough, he thought. Plenty of room for a really first-class driver. He grinned as the man jumped for life and then realized he was mistaken. The six-wheeler hit the two cars like a cork being wedged into the neck of a bottle, clutched them for a moment and then, amid shouts of abuse from their occupants and the sound of tearing metal, tore itself free and thundered on down the road.

The Children of Paul stopped at the end of the valley where an overhanging rock provided them with shade. They had heads and limbs and they walked upright. From the distance it was impossible to make out the details of their appearance, though it was clear that they were descended from men and women, but a long time ago. Apart from their faces they were covered with thick matted hair which gave them a hunched, fungoid look, and they were much taller than normal human beings. There were only eighteen of them.

'Help me, Lord.' Cold sweat was pouring down the bishop's forehead, though he didn't know why he should be frightened. The creatures under the rock did not look particularly hostile or threatening, but somehow they terrified him more than he had imagined possible. As they came down the valley, there had been an uncanny uniformity about their movements which made him feel that they were not individuals, but mindless bodies controlled by a single brain.

'Give me strength, Lord. Please give me strength.' Fenge looked at his companions. In the far distance he could hear an aeroplane, but apart from the sobbing of a child, the crowd behind him was completely silent.

'Gentlemen, I think it is time that we went over there.' The bishop had many faults, but cowardice was not one of them.

'Mr. Trant? Professor Tonks? Aren't you coming?' He saw the blank refusal in their faces and nodded. 'Very well, I shall go alone.'

'No, I will come with you, my lord.' Sir Robert Blascombe pulled himself up from his chair. 'I am not a fast walker, but with your lordship's help I can manage the distance. Thank you.' He grasped Fenge's arm and they moved off.

It was slightly over a hundred yards to the mouth of the valley and it took them a long time. Blascombe was a heavy man and now and again his feet stumbled on the uneven ground, needing all the bishop's strength to support him. As they approached, the huge figures under the crag gave no sign of recognition. They just stood there, with heads bowed far forward, hiding their faces, as though the light was troubling them.

What are they really like, Fenge wondered, as he staggered on. Over the centuries, Nature had given them telepathic powers, extreme longevity and the means to withstand their environment. But he sensed that she would have played some terrible practical jokes as well, and hideous physical deformities were hidden beneath that red matted hair. He also sensed that every one of them was old. At some period of their history, the powers of reproduction must have been lost and these few were the sole survivors of almost seven hundred years.

'Brothers – brothers and sisters.' The two men halted at the edge of the shadow cast by the rocks, but though Fenge's voice carried clearly back to the crowd, the Children of Paul stood completely motionless, with their faces sunk into their chests, apparently unaware of his presence.

'Please listen to me, brothers and sisters. We are friends who have come to welcome you – to help you. Like you we are men – men – . . .' The word echoed backwards and forwards across the crags, but there was still no sign that the hunched figures had heard him.

'You are frightened, aren't you?' A beam of sunlight glittered on the silver crosier. 'Centuries ago you were persecuted and you hid from the world. That is all over now, and there is nothing to fear any more. We are friends, come to greet you and lead you back into the love of your fellow men. This is not the end of life, but a new beginning – a wonderful beginning.' He lifted the crosier and started to make the sign of the cross.

'Bless you, my brothers and sisters. Bless you and . . .' One by one, slowly and deliberately, as though taking part in some formal, age-old ritual the creatures raised their faces into the light.

Nobody actually saw what happened after that, but every member of the crowd heard the bishop scream and all of them shared some of his agony, though in different ways. To Admiral Vane it was as if boiling water had been suddenly thrown into his face, searing the eyeballs and blinding him. When he could open his eyes again, there was some kind of commotion going on in the crowd and smoke was drifting across the moor. He knew that it was quite unimportant, as were the Children of Paul who had left the shadow of the valley and were moving out into the sunlight. Nothing mattered at all, except the strange noise in his head, and the slow but certain realization that this was the last day and he had to pay his debts; a great many debts.

With the noise in his head increasing at every second, he forced himself to turn and look at his wife. He dreaded what he expected to see, but the reality was far, far worse. Her face had become a mask of loathing, and there was the gleam of pure mania in her eyes.

You fool, he thought. You stupid blind fool! Yes, that is what she was really like all the time, and once you thought she was lovely. You gave yourself to that. He drew back as she cursed and spat at him, and the memory of every quarrel they had had in forty years joined the noise in his head.

Yes, you ruined your life for that. You put up with her canting whining religion that drove every friend we had from the house. He hardly felt her knee smash into his groin or her nails ripping open his face. He was just completely happy because he knew what she was at last, and the noise increased to a thunderous crescendo that blanked out everything except hatred and the will for revenge. This was the last day and he himself was the judge.

'You slept with that. You married that. You thought that was attractive.' He shouted at the top of his voice and his fists thudded into her body. 'You produced children with that.' She fell back against a boulder, and he saw the thing that he needed lying at her feet.

'Yes, you thought you loved that.' The jagged lump of rock was firmly embedded in the earth and it took all his strength to move it. At last it came free however, and he raised it over his shoulders.

'Love! Don't you know, Dorothy? Don't you realize that there is no such thing as love? There is only pain, and hatred and death, so die, you bitch.' Her coat was open showing the little gold crucifix at her throat, and he screamed in triumph, 'Go and die with your Jesus.'

CHAPTER NINETEEN

The track up to the moor was very steep, almost one in four at times, but in good health the lorry should have taken it in its stride. It wasn't healthy though. A manifold gasket had been fractured during the collision with the police cars and, though the exhaust noise was deafening, the engine developed far less than its normal power.

It was overheating badly too. Mott glanced at the temperature gauge. The needle was well over the normal mark and rising steadily.

'Come on, girl. Come on, my good old girl.' They were almost at the top of the hill at last. Somewhere in the distance the heather appeared to be on fire and blue smoke was drifting along the ridge.

'That's it. Only a little farther to go, and we'll be on the level.' As though in contemptuous answer to his encouragements, the needle suddenly jerked up to boiling point, and the windscreen was blanketed by steam.

'Damn!' Mott switched off the engine and applied the hand-brake. 'We'll have to let her cool down for a few minutes, but now is as good a time as any to start getting prepared. How far is it to the crags?'

'About a couple of miles.' Tom looked at the map. 'It appears to be pretty level all the way, but the track ends at the top of this hill, and you'll have to drive straight across the moors.'

'Yes, and I'll also have to get the wind behind me if something really has happened. Judging from that smoke, I'd bet my bottom dollar it has.' Mott climbed out of the cab and lifted the bonnet. Steam was still rising from the overflow pipe, but the radiator wasn't actually boiling. He opened the cap and poured in the contents of the screen-washer tank. There wasn't enough water to go far, but it should take them a couple of miles before the engine seized.

'Well, Doc, here we go.' He closed the bonnet and grinned at Tom. 'This is it, and I don't honestly know which I'm dreading the most; meeting those creatures, or finding that they don't exist. We'll have a packet to answer for if they don't. Breaking into an army depot and stealing a lorry; charging that constable and wrecking two police cars. We could be deprived of our liberty for quite some time.'

'I'm sure we could, so let's get started.' Tom pointed down the hill. Far below them a black car was hurtling along the road. The police had either made a temporary repair to one of their vehicles, or obtained reinforcements for the pursuit.

'Right you are.' Mott handed him a gas-mask and grinned again. 'Don't forget this, and all the luck in the world.' He watched Tom climb up among the cylinders and then returned to the cab. The engine started instantly, and with another thunderous blast of exhaust they lumbered up the slope.

It was only a few yards to the top, and there the track ended and the moors stretched out before them fairly level, but the surface was rough and dotted with glacial drift. Tom gripped the top of the cab as Mott changed into a higher gear and the lorry lurched forward across the heather.

There was the fence now. Rusty wire clutched at them and then snapped, and in the distance he could make out the crags. The bracken was on fire all right. Probably somebody had knocked over an oil stove, and the flames were bent in the wind with tiny figures around them. The moor must be as dry as tinder.

Yes, something had happened, there was no doubt about that. Mott was turning to the right to get the wind behind them, and though Tom couldn't make out much detail yet, he could see the crowd weren't behaving normally. Nobody was actually running from the fire, and some people appeared to be fighting. Even as he watched he saw a man being forced backwards into the flames. It was time to let loose the gas.

Tom pulled on his mask and bent over the nearest cylinder. He had already fixed the key in position and the valve turned easily, making a sharp hissing noise and releasing pale yellow vapour. The wind was in the right direction at last, and it drifted quickly towards the crags.

'Oh, my God.' The lorry topped a little ridge and Tom saw clearly what was happening. They were too late, far too late to help a lot of people.

The crowd had turned into an insane mob, and he shuddered as he looked at it. A man had brained another with a stone – a woman was thrown screaming into the fire – a child had been swung by its ankles and dashed against a rock. It was a massacre and, behind it, eighteen enormous hunched figures were moving slowly through the smoke.

'The size of them – the way they walk!' Tom muttered aloud, as the smoke thinned for a moment and he could see them clearly. He had expected the group mania in the crowd, he had expected that the creatures' appearance would be frightening, but he had never imagined that they would be so large or have that slow uniform gait like part of a ritual.

Their power was reaching him now. The valve of the next cylinder felt like ice under his fingers, and his face seemed to swell against the mask. He and Mott had fortified themselves with Drinamyl some two hours earlier, but its effects of well-being had given way to despair.

There they were again. Another gust of wind cleared the smoke and another shudder shook his body. For six hundred years, he thought, for almost seven centuries they had hidden themselves from the world. They had just one aim and one ambition and there was nothing but a deep faith and hatred to support them. Now this was the last day. The judge had revealed himself and their tainted thoughts were going out like bacteria to infect mankind.

No, nothing could stop those waves of hatred. The gas was amongst them. He could see it like a lemon-coloured mist mingling with the smoke, but it wouldn't have any effect. Their powers had been perfected over the centuries, and the only defence was by running away. Beyond the roar of the exhaust he could hear screams and shouts from the crowd. In a few minutes every human being on the moor would be dead and . . . yes, it was Mott who was responsible. Mott had given the bishop his information. Mott might well have killed Mary. Mott had brought him up here to his death. Mott was to blame for everything and his loathing of the man blacked out every other thought.

Yes, Mott. Everything was due to Mott. The lorry had increased its speed, lurching down a scree slope and throwing him back against the cylinders, but he caught a rope and somehow managed to hang on. He was about to die, but there was something he had to do first.

Tom gripped the heavy spanner in his left hand, and crawled

forward, lowering himself over the side boards till he could reach the handle of the cab door. The lorry was zigzagging madly, as though Mott were trying to shake him off, but he had to hang on. Mott must be killed and every boast and insult would be paid in full. The door opened and he lifted the spanner and swung it like a flail at Mott's forehead.

He couldn't have been unconscious for more than a few seconds, that was certain. The lorry had crashed against a boulder, throwing him clear, and one of its front wheels was off the ground and still revolving. Tom stared stupidly at it and then pulled himself to his feet, wincing as he did so. He must have sprained his ankle in the fall, and all hatred had left him, and he felt nothing except pain and a sense of complete bewilderment. In front of him the air was a thick haze of smoke and escaping gas, and behind, the noise of the crowd had decreased; shouts and screams turned to a low collective whimper. The fire was only a few yards away, but with the wind behind it there was no danger there.

Gritting his teeth against the pain from his ankle, Tom staggered forward. Mott lay sprawled senseless beside the cab of the lorry. His gas-mask had been torn off when he fell, and he was bleeding from a gash on his temple. He didn't seem to be in any danger, though. The pulse was practically normal, and judging by the eyes, there was no concussion. He took off his jacket to make a pillow for Mott's head, and as he did so, a sudden gust of wind cleared the smoke and he stiffened.

He had forgotten, of course. Following his fall, he had only thought about Mott and the change in the crowd, and he had forgotten that the danger remained. Behind the fire a group of tall figures were standing.

Yes, the creatures were still active all right. He judged, from his own reactions and those of the crowd, that the gas had checked their telepathic powers, but certainly not their power of will. Though the smoke hid their faces, he knew they would be contorted with hatred.

They were turning towards him. All together they swung slowly round and began to move forward, as though realizing who their real enemies were. The heather and bracken were bone dry and the wind was whipping up the flames, but the fire wasn't much of a barrier. It came to an end a few yards to his left, and all they had to do was to walk around it.

Tom opened the bonnet of the lorry and pulled out the starting-handle. Mott was still unconscious and there was no chance of moving him in time. He had tried to kill him and now he would probably have to die for him. He stationed himself with his back against the radiator, waiting for them to turn and walk round the fire. As he did so, the smoke thinned and he saw them clearly.

Their faces were ravaged by age and disease and, unlike the rest of their bodies, completely hairless. At either side of the skull, external tumours reared up to give them the appearance of horned devils, but that wasn't their most repulsive feature. From each swollen jaw and cheek and forehead hung things like scarlet ribbons – things that moved with a life of their own.

'The Gorgon – the snakes of the Gorgon.' Tom gasped in horror, seeing the legend become fact before his eyes, and he knew that their will to destroy had been supported by physical pain as well as faith. Almost all creatures carry parasites, and the Children of Paul had housed a monster. Their flesh was honeycombed and from some of the holes, drawn out by light or heat, worms as thick as matchsticks were crawling.

They were getting close – very close. Fifteen yards from the edge of the fire – ten. Surely they must be feeling the heat now? They had to turn and go around it. Seven yards – six – five. Tom suddenly knew hope again.

For, by heaven, they weren't turning! They were still coming on, striding straight into a clump of blazing bracken. Either their senses had been dulled by the gas or, over the centuries, they had forgotten the nature of fire. He felt pity as well as hope now, because they were obviously in agony: their bodies twisting convulsively, though they made no sound. Telepathy must have removed the need for speech and the vocal cords atrophied.

They were stopping at last: tongues of flame running up their legs and stripping away hair to show the monstrous deformities it had hidden. One after the other they halted in the centre of the fire, and some were clutching at the flames, as though they imagined them to be solid objects which could be pulled aside. The wind veered slightly and Tom smelled the stench of the pit mingling with that of burning flesh and hair.

Not all had stopped, though. The one in front which had some sort of metal band around its right arm was still coming on – marching across the blazing earth, as though pain was beneath its contempt. Worms were dropping from the wrinkled cheeks, and above them Tom could see the huge, pale eyes flash with hatred. The creature had spent all its incredibly long life waiting for this single day and it would carry out the crusade of destruction till the bitter end.

It was almost through the fire now. The charred feet were stepping on to blackened heather, and the body appeared to straighten and swell in triumph. Tom raised the crank handle, but it was like a toy against the thing that was coming – the thing which was out of its tomb at last and coming straight for him. Striding across the ground, vast, monstrous, but also strangely pathetic, with the eyes glaring down at him from the ravaged face and arms stretched rigidly forward.

He struck out with the crank, but long taloned fingers wrenched it from his grasp and hurled him against the lorry. They were within inches of his throat when another sharp gust of wind suddenly whistled over the moor and fanned the smouldering hair till it flared like a torch.

For perhaps ten seconds, but to Tom they could have been hours, the creature stood swaying before him. Then the hands clenched together in a completely human gesture of despair, the knees started to buckle and it staggered backwards into the fire.

CHAPTER TWENTY

It was late afternoon. All the wounded and most of the dead had been taken away. Even the few reporters allowed on the moor were beginning to leave, though a newsreel helicopter still hovered over the crags. Mott smiled at Tom and Mary. His left eye was black and there was a strip of sticking plaster across his forehead.

'Well, that's it. All's well that ends well, and we can go home.'

'All's well?' Mary frowned as another ambulance lurched past them. As soon as the news of the massacre broke, a police car had taken her to the moor and she had half-expected to find that Tom was dead. The scene on her arrival had been like a nightmare. People were just throwing off the effects of the gas and starting to realize what had happened: the wounded screaming in agony – others discovering that they had killed their loved ones – some still insane; the bishop crawling in circles, a helpless imbecile, with Robert Blascombe's blood and hair sticking to his crosier. A woman who had killed her child was holding her hands into the fire. Admiral Vane . . .

No, his story had a happy ending. Mary had found him sitting beside his wife with tears pouring down his cheeks. 'Can you forgive me, Dot?' he had kept saying. 'Can you ever forgive me? In just another second, I would have killed you. Please try and under-stand, my darling. I was suddenly driven mad. I didn't know what I was doing.' His face had lit up like a child's when she smiled at him.

'Of course I forgive you, George. We were both insane, weren't we? I would have killed you if I'd had the strength. But now it's all over.' An ambulance man had beckoned to them and the two old people got up and walked away hand in hand.

'Yes, Mary, though there has been a lot of death and suffering, we didn't come off too badly.' Mott watched the helicopter make a final circuit of the moor before turning south to Tynecastle. He was feeling very pleased with himself, imagining future headlines, and books, and television interviews. Only he had had the courage and intelligence to defeat those creatures, and he had done so against opposition from the Church, the police and the army. He had made that quite clear to several journalists, and the morning papers should make very pleasant reading indeed. He grinned at Tom.

'You gave me quite a clout with that spanner, old boy, but don't reproach yourself. I tried to kill you on the way down: swerving the lorry in the hope of throwing you off. Until you laid me out, your death seemed to be the one important thing there was.'

'Yes, death was the important thing, because this was the Day of Judgment.' Tom looked at the valley again, as though half expecting to see another group of figures stationed under the crags.

'Before, they used their powers as a means of self-defence, but this was the last day when man would be taught to hate and destroy his neighbour. Not an inefficient way to end the world.

'But I still can't see how they managed to keep it up.' Mary followed his stare. The nearest rocks were warm and pleasant in the sunlight, but the valley itself was in shadow and made her think of a gaping mouth.

'Oh, I can understand how the physical changes were produced by environment and inbreeding and that horrible disease. I can also understand a little about their telepathic powers. But the length of time that they went on hating! Almost seven hundred years!'

'Pain had a lot to do with it, I imagine.' Tom remembered those scarlet ribbons he had seen crawling out from the ravaged flesh. 'They were obviously suffering from something like Dracontiasis, Guinea Worm: one of the most painful illnesses known to man, but not a quick killer. Probably they became infected by eating raw fish, and the same diet gave them the power to live with it. The carp is one of the longest-lived animals, but it also carries an abnormal number of parasites. Constant agony over generations might be quite a spur to hatred.'

'There's also the matter of deep faith.' Mott broke in pompously. 'When I first heard about the Children of Paul, I imagined them to be one of the usual crazy but harmless sects, so common during the Middle Ages. Then, I noticed the dates, and began to wonder who the judge they were expecting really was. Remember that they went down into the caves in 1300, and were to remain there for exactly six hundred and sixty-six years.' The sun was very hot and he pulled out a handkerchief and wiped his forehead.

'Before long, a party of brave young men will go down to explore their hiding place, and I think they will find drawings and other records to tell us a good deal about that judge. Don't ask me to accompany them, though. I wouldn't set foot in those caves for all the gold at Fort Knox.

'If we go over there, I may be able to show you something

rather significant, however.' He led them across to the wrecked lorry. Most of the bodies in front of it had been removed, but three still lay stretched out on the sodden ground. The fire brigade had used a lot of water and wreaths of steam were rising around them. They looked far smaller and less formidable in death, but Mary had to force herself to go near.

'Firstly, I'd like you to note that there were eighteen – exactly eighteen.

'Just a moment please, gentlemen.' Mott waved back a party of ambulance men. 'If more existed, as appears likely to me, I think they were killed in the caves. You see, it was essential that only that number should come out on the last day.'

'But why? What's so special about eighteen?' Tom stared down at the monstrous, charred figure before him, its mouth wide open, as though screaming in agony, and the teeth incredibly old and worn right down to the gums.

'Don't you know, Doc? You should spend more time with your Bible. The Book of Revelation – Chapter 13, if I remember rightly.' Mott knelt down and lifted an enormous arm. The circlet around it was of dull red gold, and though worn by time and distorted by fire, the carved symbols were still visible. A T shape with globes hanging under the bar, and three Roman numerals.

'Yes, this makes it pretty clear who they thought their judge would be. The one who "shall ascend out of the bottomless pit and go into perdition."' Mott twisted the amulet into the light. 'That is a Tau cross, one of the very earliest anti-Christian symbols, and these . . .' he pointed to the numerals. 'According to Saint John the Divine, "6 6 6" is the Number of the Beast.'

'I suppose you are right. It must have taken something as horrible as that to support them.' Tom gave a final glance at the thing on the ground and turned away.

'Yes, nearly seven centuries, but at last it's over. The curse has left this village and we can go home. Come on, darling.' He took Mary's arm and they walked off to the waiting cars.

ALSO AVAILABLE FROM VALANCOURT BOOKS

CPSIA information can be obtained
at www.ICGtesting.com
Printed in the USA
LVHW041312060219
606576LV00001B/366

9 781941 147108